A Map to the Stars

Ashley Hutchison

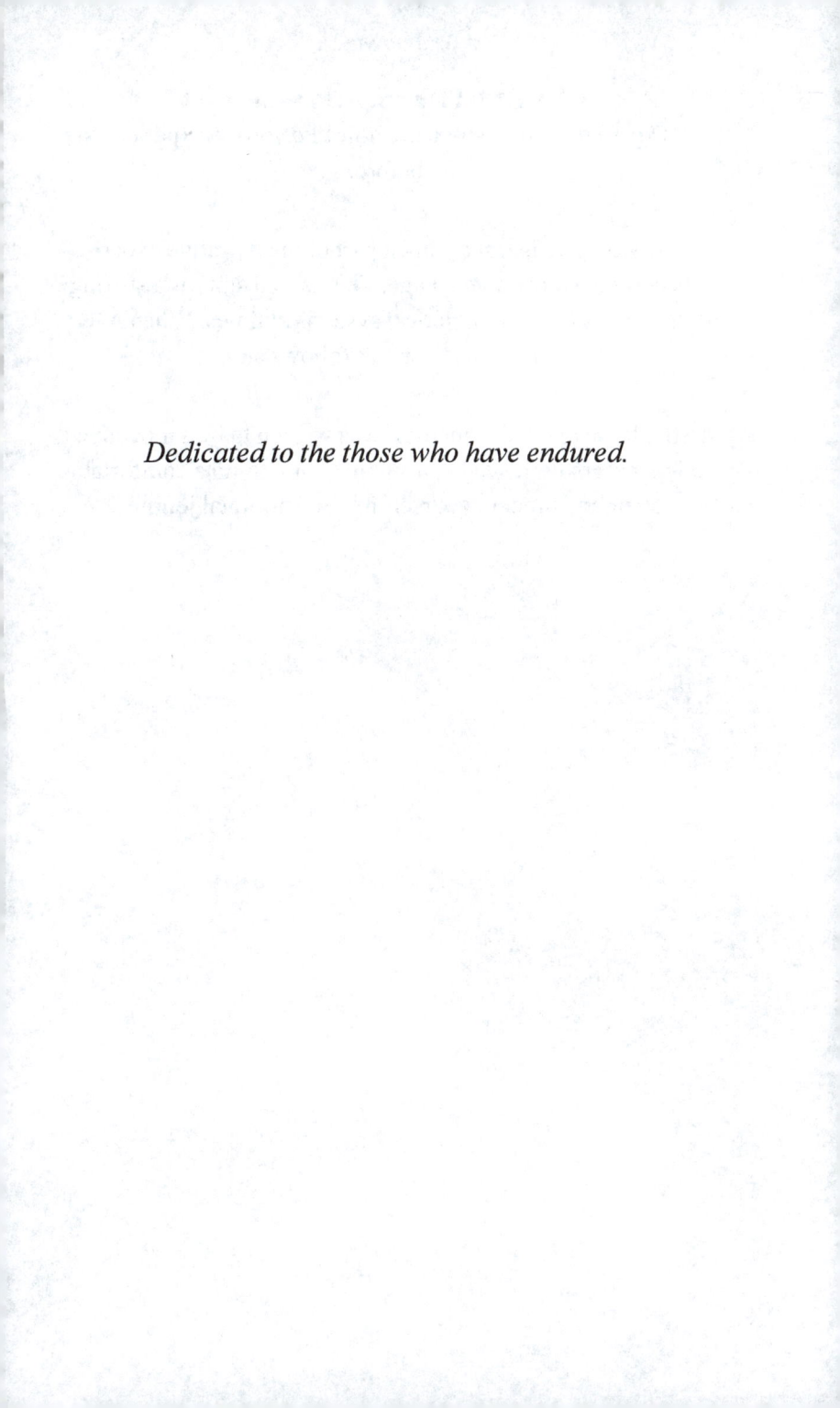

Dedicated to the those who have endured.

REVELATIONS, before the first
A Map to the Stars isn't a memoir like you've experienced before.

The structure is just as much part of the narrative experience as the words on the page. This sacred story is a stirring thing and ignores grammatical systems at times. When Avery unravels, the book follows suit.

Also, please know this memoir was written to be a movement, so it is best experienced in a single sitting. Find a comfortable chair and prepare yourself for an emotional journey.

In the Beginning...

(Age: 0-5)

There was a house. A house on a hill overlooking a church. A house on a hill with willow trees planted just for her. A house on a hill with a wooden swing made just for her. A grey house on a hill overlooking a church. It was grey on the outside, but not on the inside. Inside was magic. Inside was love.

The inside was occupied by furniture, none of which matched. The inside was occupied by hard carpet and strange floors that weren't level. The inside was occupied by people.

Family.

Her family.

A little girl, her grandmother, her grandfather, and her aunt. Family. Magic, and love, and family. At one time the little girl's mother was there with them, but she had gone away. She was with a husband and another little girl. Her sister, they called her. The little girl often wondered why her family wasn't her mother and her new husband and her new little girl. But being with her family at the grey house on the hill overlooking the church with the willow trees planted just for her and a wooden swing made just for her was perfect.

Anytime she remembered it as she grew up, she would think of climbing into the sink to watch her aunt outside from the window. She would throw bread over the fence in the backyard for the birds. Then she would come back inside and the two would watch as the birds flew in. They would try to name each kind.

She would remember the age of her grandfather's hands. He called her "precious jewel" and "sugarplum". She would remember her grandmother searching for her all over the house when they played hide-and-seek. She would remember it all bathed in the yellow and orange hues of sunset.

It would end. The little girl named Avery would have to leave this place of magic, and love, and family. Her mother would come for her. It would be the only time in Avery's life that she came for her.

There was a grey house on the hill overlooking the church with willow trees planted just for her and a wooden swing made just for her, and she never saw it again.

PART I:

THE MOTHER

I was hers. I was hers and she was mine and for such a tragically brief time we belonged to one another completely. We were held together by the force of each other's gravity, so heavily influenced by the passing moods we exhibited. All things for us began and ended with the other. She was Alpha and I, Omega. And because we were so tied it was all the more lamentable when our cord of communion was broken.

She and he joined. She and he joined, coupled, and from their union she bore him another. This new one was entirely different, red and erupting, with violence flowing about her surface. No longer was I the place where the sun rose and set in her vision, and our sacred, perfect bond was invaded. These intruders interrupted our united gravity so, and I saw her own weakening under theirs. Both of them dominant, demanding, and oppressive. In her diminished state, I watched as her core changed. What was once a center of soft, warm ivory, became that of cracked, gray iron. The change in her core caused a poison to spread its death to her landscape, robbing it of its vibrancy. In time all she offered was stolen from her. In time, she was barren.

When at last the change in her was complete, the two invaders drew together and overcame her, so that she and I were at last separated. Our singular bond was severed. The break was so jarring, so abrupt that I was cast out of this system and was sent hurtling into the dark unknown, thoroughly damaged from my loss. My view of her as I was thrown out was eclipsed so that I was unable to transmit any sense of this loss I felt to her. I saw only the dominant ones, and my view of the three became smaller as I was pulled, pulled again by another, an alien force of gravity that was many light-years away. But I felt it all the same.

As I passed through the new space, I saw many systems. So many of them connected harmoniously and so I wondered at my own system and how it came to be so calamitous. Possibly it was that my core and those of the invaders were extraordinarily polar. I had not long to examine theirs as I had hers, for we seemed to have always been, uninterrupted in that way, for a length of time I could not comprehend. My core and hers had been so remarkably similar that it was plain for any observer to see that I had been born of her side, of her materials. But the other one she had borne, had inherited nothing of her, none of her minerals.

I again felt the pull of that strange gravity. This time, stronger. I even noticed changes within my own landscape as it came closer, and I shifted into a new phase in my life cycle. I felt the pull, but my face never changed direction. My gaze was fixed backwards, longing, despairing at the loss of her, of she who bore me. I had known her, and she had known me, so deeply, so perfectly that our shared gravities had created a hum, a vibration of harmony. I could not shake her memory, and so I resolved that my core would remain unchanged. A soft, warm ivory that used to match hers. It would not be stolen from me. She would remain below my surface, at my center throughout the ages.

Revelations: The First

I was six-years old when I thought about death for the first time.

My grandmother died and I put a red rose on her chest at the wake.

It was her favorite flower.

I didn't understand. She was lying there, but she didn't look the same. Her features were wax-like, as if it were not her, but a representation of her. A likeness. Her skin was stretched too thin across her face. And she was cold. Her hand was cold.

My mother wasn't there. They never really got along.

I was angry with my mother. She had no reason good enough for her absence.

There was someone so special lying in front of me who had once put magic and sweetness into my life. And now all of that was stuffed into a box. They would put her in the ground.

And the red rose on her chest would be locked in the darkness with her.

They told me she wasn't coming back. They said she had gone to heaven.

Where is heaven? Does anyone know?

I hate my mother.

I hate roses.

I remember waking up suddenly. I remember hearing the shouting outside of Blair's and my bedroom door. I remember climbing out of bed and quickly jumping into Blair's bed. I remember her crying and asking me what was happening. I remember putting my arms around her neck, my fingers stroking her cheeks. I remember telling her that everything was all right. We will be safe.

I remember the banging sounds. Glass breaking. I remember our bedroom door swinging open. I remember the look on my mother's face. I remember her tears. I remember her telling Blair and me that we were not staying in this house anymore. I remember him shouting behind her. I could feel her fear.

I remember thinking that this was what war must be like. I remember everything in flashes. I remember my sister's nightgown. I remember the ducks on it and how it trembled as her body trembled while we moved from one corner of the room to the other, gathering our most important items.

I don't remember whose car we got into when my mother made us pack and leave. I don't remember the words she said as we all piled into the strange car with the strange, new man. I don't remember how much we cried that night, but I bet it could be measured in buckets.

I remember this scene replaying over and over and over. I remember every house we left.

Confession

I saw it all, mom. Each time you moved us from man to man I saw it all.

I saw the bruises you carelessly hid, saw you smoking cigarette after cigarette in every different kitchen, one after the other. I saw you press them angrily into an ashtray or the table, whichever was available. Then I saw you slide your head into your hands, your red nails bright against your chocolate-colored hair, and you would cry. I saw you from behind the doorway where I would always sit when you cried. Just out of eyesight, I would sit with you.

I stayed behind the doorways when I heard the screams. And when I heard the crashes and thuds. *So much anger, and for what? Why was it always the same?* Each man you brought us to wore a different face, though was possessed by the same evil.

Once, I saw a soda bottle crash against the wall. It was meant for your face.

Another time, I saw you being pushed against a wall, hands twisting your wrists.

I'll kill you bitch! I'll kill you! I'll kill you! I'll kill you!

I stayed behind the doorways just on the precipice of hell. You were terrified. I was too. While they gave you bruises that the world could see, I was given ones I could hide better than you. Maybe you thought you were alone, *but you were not.*

I stayed behind the doorways. Just out of eyesight, I would sit with you.

I was eleven. I was only eleven when you brought me to him.

Lance

She remembered the first time he came for her.

It was only a few months earlier.
The man who belonged to her mother.
He came at her;
looking at her hungrily with ice-blue eyes.
He chased her through the house and into the bathroom.
Her stomach bunched up, turning to knots.
She was only eleven years old.
She was afraid.

His face changed.
His walk was different.
He reached towards her, no longer a man, but a demon
a monster with ice-blue eyes.
She felt herself shrinking
smaller and smaller.
She wanted to disappear.

He grabbed a handful of her hair
and she tried to scream.
She closed her eyes.
She was a great warrior
who wore such armor as no one could pierce.
The sun shining on her face.
Her bruises, gone.

Her pain, faded.
For this time, she was untouchable.
For this moment, she was unbreakable.

He left her there.
This time she heard the footsteps
pounding on the floor as he came for her.
She found a corner in her room and curled up.
She waited knowing no escape.
Her hands found each other around her head.

The door was opened; the rope and tape he held
found their way around her; surrounded her.
She thought she might die this way.

He put her somewhere dark.
While she cried for her mother.
No one came. No one heard.
She closed her eyes.
She was a great warrior
who wore such armor as no one could pierce.
The sun shining on her face.
Her bruises, gone.
Her pain, faded.
For a time, she was untouchable.
In this moment, at least, she was unbreakable.

I hate you mom. *How could you let him touch me?*
You know he touched me. The demon with the ice-blue
eyes. Those eyes I can't ever get out of my head.

I hate you. *He dragged me into the bathroom one*
day, and the next day he tied me up and left me in a
closet for four hours. I screamed for you. I cried out
and called your name. Why didn't you come?

I fucking hate you. *You said you would protect*
me. You said you would make sure he paid for it. You
took him to court and told me it was for me. But you
were suing him for keeping your stupid fucking scuba
gear.

Why didn't you protect me? *His fingers*
left their marks on me. They are there, always, invisible
to everyone but me. I see them every time I look in a
mirror.

His hands ripped away my innocence.

The 9 Theses that really felt like 95:

You couldn't stand to be around me. Was I such a nuisance to you that you had to dump me with whatever family member would take me in? I didn't see you for months at a time. Once, when I was in the third grade, you left me with one of my aunts for three years. You have no idea what that felt like.

You let me believe for ten years that the same man who fathered my sister was mine too. You will never understand how confusing it was for me to then be separated from the three of you, when I believed so strongly that I belonged with you and those two. What was so wrong with me that I couldn't be with you three?

After your divorce from my sister's father, you lost your sense of direction. You dragged us from place to place, letting each man you clung to beat you, traumatize you, and humiliate you. Sometimes Blair and I saw it, sometimes we only heard. You let it happen all the same.

You let that man, the one with the ice-blue eyes.

You let

You failed me.

The most important man in my life passed away when I was fourteen, and you didn't bother to tell me that he died. My grandfather was the only father I've ever known – and you couldn't bother to tell me he died.

I disappeared into the woods after I heard the news on the telephone with my aunt. I was gone for forever it seemed, crying and sleeping in the trees.

It was the same year that my grandfather passed away that I experienced what exploitation felt like. It was by your hand. Though your efforts failed, the fact that I was nearly sold into marriage to an older man only amplified my suffering. I realized then that my existence was only tolerated when I was considered advantageous to you.

But you still were able to surprise me.

It seems like something out of a bad fantasy book for angsty teens, but it was all too real. You were lost to me, to everyone. You became engrossed in darkness and dark things and declared that I would bear the Anti-Christ at some point in my life.

I was terrified. You were so alien to me that I no longer recognized in you the core which bonded us. You were gone. And I knew I had to be gone too.

But *gone* didn't come until you took the first boy I ever loved. He was sixteen and I was fifteen and you were thirty-five. My virginity belonged to him, but his innocence belonged to you. The hunter hunted and in its own lust to devour it forgot to think of those left behind to endure the pain it left in its wake.

Gone came when I saw him crying over what you'd taken from him.

The ultimate *gone* – the transformation of *gone* into *vanished utterly* – came soon after the *gone*. The boy I loved carried me away so that I might become part of his family. For a heartbeat, your ruse of maternal instinct and love fooled me. But I overheard your conversation with the surrogates. You would abandon me easily if the surrogates would allow you to keep the child support you received from my father.

A price on my head. If anyone wants to know my worth, it was five-hundred dollars a month. Six thousand dollars a year. Eighteen thousand dollars total. Well, at least then I knew *how much* you valued my custody.

Vanished utterly came.

But I still remember you.

Before I loved a boy, before I was the subject of your fear, before I learned of the big lie and all of the little ones, and before your ice-blue eyed man…well, before him, I remember our matching cores. A time when you and I were so alike, and you were such a mother whose laughter was so deafeningly joyous that its sound still reverberates in the pulses of my temples and the tunnels of my bones.

Their relationship is like a shit-stained, golden dress...

Her fingers created. She was astonishing in that way. A painter, a sculptor, a seamstress. So much splendor was born from the finesse of her hands. Avery could not help but admire all that her mother might be. All that she was. All that emanated from her spongy insides as she worked with steely determination and the fiery mania that made great artists great.

Halloween costumes were never bought. Ever. A headless bride, a cereal killer, Hellraiser. They were all the master-pieces of those hands of hers. But Avery was exhausted of horror. She was tired of carrying around mannequin heads or spending hours watching her sister have dozens of pins glued to her face under a bathing cap. Avery wanted just once to be a princess.

Of course her mother didn't approve. Horror was her stock and trade. Horror was the genre of her life. So it must too be her daughter's.

Avery begged.

Begged.

Begged.

Carried around more mannequin heads.

Begged a little more.

She caved the year before Avery was set to enter middle school. Avery felt happiness as a butterfly in her belly, too young to understand that the flutter of its wings against the lining of her stomach was a warning. Too young. Too happy.

Avery lost herself in the swirl of golden fabric and the reluctant willingness of her mother. There was finally understanding. They had finally bridged the gap torn open by horror. Avery had never looked more beautiful. Neither had her mother. Their smiles were wider, and their laughter was sweeter.

The night before Halloween the golden dress fell from its hanger in the closet that was left open. The next morning Avery discovered the dog that belonged to her mother's boyfriend had shit all over it.

Shit and gold.
That shit never gets old

PART II:

THE SISTER

(Age: 27)

Revelations: The Second

I remember a conversation we had not too long ago

a brief connection after so much

time spent apart.

We spoke of the changes in our lives, but we couldn't forever the subject of my departure. You wanted to understand why I left. I just couldn't tell you. After that you were gone.

Such an empty word.

gone.

My dear sister. I could not bear to tell you why I left because I knew it could destroy your perceived sweetness of *her.*

The only way that I can explain it to you best is by saying this:

Blair, we have two different mothers.

I feel I must elaborate on that, as I am aware that it must sound strange since genetically, we were born of the same woman's body, but not of the same person. We underwent many of the same tragedies that were the result of our mother's choices, though we experienced them differently, they altered us differently.

Your mother accepted and appreciated your stubbornness, your brash and sometimes abrasive personality. No matter how intelligent you were, you never had to strive or actually achieve anything since your grades were never the subject of severe scrutiny. Your mother clung to you, your mother protected you, your mother kept you from hurt.

Our mother *loved you because you were all that she became.*

No matter how well I was performing in school, I never received slack nor praise. I was shown all the worst of our mother and was pushed towards destruction for the simple fact that *I was all that she was* before abuse twisted her, mangled her, pressed her into a new form. *I was the sore reminder of what was lost.*

My heart is breaking as I write this. I am afraid of the power of these words. I fear that the sweet image of your mother will dissolve into unforgiving reality, and I don't wish that for you. I wish for you to keep your sweet mother, and if my sacrifice is that I must no longer speak with you, it is a sacrifice which I am most willing to make.

But I still love you.

I still think of you.

I still miss our unusual bond.

I still can't forgive myself for leaving you.

We redefined ourselves.

    We did – my sister and I

    through the experiences we shared,

    and through those entirely our own.

We redefined ourselves

    as our mother's whims carried

    and scattered us like wind –

    one place – another place.

    So many new faces.

We redefined ourselves.

    We grew and created – she and I.

    We wrote about secret worlds

    with secret people with secret

    secrets of their own.

    We became writers at seven and nine.

We redefined ourselves

    as we were pulled apart.

    I to my aunt and her to her father.

    I was alone – she grew harder and I grew softer.

    I painted, she played guitar.

    We became artists – though not of the same kind.

    All of this at only eleven and nine.

We redefined ourselves.

    One more move – one final chance together.

    We encountered a gulf between us too

    hard to traverse.

    We were so far from our shared beginning.

We were still both writers,
still artists of a different kind.
But while she grew harder, I grew
softer, and we were no longer
seven and nine.

In nearly every aspect the two sisters were the antithesis of the other – Blair was a tiger. Cunning, unforgiving, and possessing a quick mind which lacked a civility censor. She had such an inherent ferocity, as if she had lived as a Viking shield-maiden or an Amazon warrior in a life long before this one. Sharp, barbarous remarks that caused remarkable wounds were her weapons of choice, and these weapons she normally wielded against her sister. Everything she was came bottled in a tall, curvy figure with a mop of thick, curly brown hair and a clover-shaped nose she received from her father.

Avery owned quite a different type of strength: perseverance. She dragged herself bleeding, sobbing, or undeniably broken from one year to the next, too terrified to ever be comfortable in happiness of any kind, but also too frightened to abandon the quest for it. Her surface was misleading. Avery appeared serene without the slightest hint of turmoil underneath. Unlike Blair, Avery exhibited an effortless charisma that won her many friends and admirers. And though those who surrounded her greatly adored her, she would never share herself with anyone. She was a slave to her darker memories. She hauled her pain along with her, afraid that without it her identity would be lost. An identity which she had pieced together for herself. She wrapped herself in her heartache and wore it as armor.

Both girls had but a few things in common: they dearly loved to read and to write. This appreciation for literature was the common ground upon which they nurtured their relationship. They read and discussed the same books, both wishing to live in the world of *Harry Potter* or to reside in the pages created by Jane Austen. The two edited each other's poetry and short stories. They reveled in their own secret literary world and its magical brilliance shut out the horrors around them. And for however long they were able to remain in their secret world, the darkness did not exist. It was strangled, suffocated, stifled into absolute silence by the happiness their special bond brought to one another... especially Avery. She soaked up these happy moments like a dying flower starving for water, slaking her thirst in a great rainstorm.

Except for the times when they escaped into their secret world together, Blair and Avery were otherwise strangers. They did not understand one another and frequently argued as a result. Many times, these arguments became physical. Avery often withdrew even though she was the eldest. Avery still bore scars from Blair's fingernails on her hands that were the result of a fight between Blair and herself. She was unable to recall the reason for the argument, but she bore the scares all the same, preferring to think of them as a keepsake. Those would always belong to her and to Blair.

(Age: 15)

Avery heard the computer chair in the living room squeak. It was a reminder of the pressing task at hand. She quickly grabbed her floppy disks, which contained every one of her sacred literary creations and put them into the suitcase she had stolen from her mother's closet.

"Did...Mom, did you–" Avery *forced the question from her throat as she felt it collapse in her neck.*

Her mother, sitting on the naked mattress, looked at Avery. Guilt saturated every pore on her face and polluted her large, almond-shaped brown eyes.

When her lips began to move, she simply said, "Yes."

Avery heard nothing else. She felt her bones crack and shatter as the pain moved through her body, freezing her blood. Her soul, which used to be so vibrant and abstract and warm, withered under the weight of her mother's words.

Avery shook her head in an attempt to loosen the memory from her mind.

My clothes. I need some clothes.

She went to her closet as quickly and as quietly as possible. Avery knew that she could not draw attention to herself. This was a critical moment, and one wrong move could bring her plans crumbling around her feet. Her mind was racing so fast that at times she forgot what she was looking for. A toothbrush, her shoes, her countless drawings...the items seemed to blur together as she raced from one room to the other.

Matt came into the room just as Avery was closing her suitcase. "Are you ready?"

Avery nodded.

"Okay, we need to go...like now."

"I have to leave a note," Avery protested.

"Be quick." He kissed her. "It's okay. This is the right thing."

Avery let Matt take her suitcase through the house, carefully avoiding the living room by exiting through the den.

This is it.

Avery did not even take a moment to look around the room. She found a sheet of paper in her desk drawer and a pen, and then furiously scribbled on the paper. She remembered writing 'goodbye' but nothing else. Avery walked down the hallway, through the den, and came into the kitchen – the last stop before her escape. She placed the note on the counter by the sink.

Then, she looked up. Blair's gaze was still fixed on the computer screen as it had been all morning. Avery could see nothing of her except for the mop of brown curls falling down the back of her head all the way to the middle of her back where her hair met the distressed, red chair which belonged to the equally distressed computer table in front of her.

Avery bit her lip until it bled. She didn't know if she was trying to subdue the nausea bubbling in her belly or if it was simply her habit resurfacing under the boulder-like weight of her anxiety. There was not enough time to think. There was only enough time to do. All of Avery's emotions would have to be suppressed behind that wall she had constructed deep within her body when she was much younger. Everything behind it she knew might someday destroy her, but she couldn't worry about that now. Now, the only thing Avery allowed herself to do was to quietly and quickly memorize the way Blair looked sitting at that desk in the living room.

The sound of Matt's car in the driveway outside did not startle her. She was expecting it, though she did not welcome it. Too many things were unknown with her leaving – what she would find and what would happen to everything she left behind. Avery was afraid of her mother, afraid for her sister.

It was time to go. It was time to go. It was time to leave with her boyfriend. It was time to leave her sister behind. A gnawing hollowness ached under her ribs as she looked once more at those brown curls. Hints of lighter hues found their way into each sideways turn of a loop. The urge to retch was growing.

Avery knew she was hard at work on a new story, a new world. One she would never get to experience, to edit, to share.

Their shared time was done.

She couldn't say goodbye. *She'll tell. I'll never make it.*

She couldn't say goodbye.

I wanted so much to say goodbye. I wanted so much to take you with me.

I have never forgiven myself for leaving you.

(Age: 32)

Understanding: An exercise in futility...

Blair: Avery, you are my sister. I have always and will continue to love you for the entirety of my life. But you almost broke me when you left, and everything that happened after did the rest of the job. I want a relationship with you, but you put the restriction out that I can only have that if we don't talk about what happened. I cannot do that. I needed answers, and you would not give them to me. That is the only reason I have not been in contact with you. The only reason I haven't tried to pursue a mend to our relationship. I think and worry about you all the time, and it breaks my heart to not know my nephews.

Avery: All I have ever thought about was you. Leaving you is the one thing I have never been able to forgive myself for, but I would hate myself forever if I told you everything. You love our mother so much, and I do too, but what happened between us is so painful. Not only for me, but it would be for you too. And I've not spoken of it to spare you that because I love you. I've written so many letters to you over the years that I've never been able to send. I'd rather you hate me than me be the one to destroy anything you have with our mother.

Blair: Ignorance is always worse. Always. There is a part of me that is stuck in grief. I can't move on or heal, because the only answer I have is that you didn't love us enough to stay. And that is too painful to try to work through, so I just compartmentalized it. You are right though, I do love our mother fiercely. And there isn't a damn thing that will ever change that. But I love you just the same. I have never hated you. I am not capable of it. I have only ever been disappointed and hurt.

Avery: I didn't love you enough to stay? I would hate that you would think that to be true, because I've loved you my whole life, whether we were fighting or not. I wanted so much to grab you and take you with me, but I couldn't. Your dad would have come after you. I am so sorry that I caused you to feel that way. I wish that I would have known a way to do things differently, but I was doing what was best. I was too young to properly deal with everything that happened, and I handled it as well as I could at the time. If you need answers, then I am willing to give them to you regardless of how afraid I am of how you might respond to everything.

Blair: Why did you run away?

Avery: Are you certain that this is something you want

to discuss via text?

Blair: I don't know if I can handle talking to you yet. Through text, I can at least process before I respond.

Avery: Okay.

Avery: It was never really just one thing, there were many things over years that made me distance myself from our mother. I don't know if you care to hear about those, but I will tell you if you want me to, except for one, and that I will not say via text.

Avery: Regardless of whether or not our mother considered Matt and me to be dating, we were. But, honestly, it's not even an important thing. She bought Matt things, took him places, gave him attention. No one thought anything of it. At least, not that I am aware of. Then, one day, I caught him crying on the bathroom floor. This is what he told me: he spoke to our mother to get her approval for dating me. She told him she didn't allow me to date. Sometime during the course of their conversation they began drinking together. A lot, apparently. She had sex with him. I know it's probably going to be a gut-reaction for you to deny that it happened, and I wouldn't blame you. You and our mother have had quite a different relationship than she and I had. But I confronted her about it with Farrah, and she admitted it to both of us. After I left, she began denying it. The reason I left is not so easily summed up, but this event was certainly the last straw in a line of things.

Blair: So you believe that she raped him? Or just that they had sex?

Avery: He was 16. It was rape.

Blair: Our mother, a survivor of multiple assaults and rapes throughout her life, exhibited predatory behavior on a 16 year old, intentionally got both herself and him drunk (by your implication), and then knowingly raped him? And within the couple of months that would be the longest time frame for these events, he managed to overcome the shame and humiliation and self-loathing almost all rape survivors experience (men more so than anyone), to talk about it very casually with his girlfriend and her sister in the room? Yes, I do find that very hard to believe. Now, I will not say that there is no way that the two of them had sex, but the sequence of events that you're giving me, with all of the implications? No, I don't believe it. I remember that conversation, and knowing what I know now and the life

experiences I've had… I don't believe he
was sincere. I cannot deny that you believe it,
I have no right to your thoughts and opinions,
But I don't agree with them. You said that
that event was just the last. What were the
others? And I should clarify that the reason
I do not find Matt credible is because,
what I remember of him was a guy
that tried to walk in on me changing a few
times and asking me once if you and I ever
"double up" in dating. And with the leering,
I'm pretty sure he wasn't talking about
double dates.

Avery: Please, don't take this the wrong way, but you
asked me why I left. You wanted to know the
everything. Here I am, opening up to you and
telling you what I experienced. We cannot move
forward if your plan is to pick apart everything I
tell you, because it's not going to help. Whether
or not Matt was a sleezebag, and whether or not
he wanted to have sex with our mother is 100%
irrelevant. He was 16. It was rape. I'm not
harboring ill feelings toward our mother simply
because I believe that she "stole my boyfriend"
or something. The fact remains that she was the
adult in the situation and she chose to have
sex with a child. If you want to move forward

with me and us try to mend our relationship, you can't try to hammer down everything I say, because I'm only telling you my side of the story.

Blair: I'm not trying to be combative or hammer you, I am trying to have a dialogue. If all you want is to say your piece with little to no rebuttal from me then I can do that. And I'm not angry with what you're saying, I'm skeptical. And please don't think for a moment that I have our mother on a pedestal: I know her. She is just as flawed and fucked up as I am. But she was also there for us, working herself to exhaustion to provide for us, with no help from either of our fathers. That's the mother I remember, even with all her broken places, she did her best for us. Maybe you don't see her that way, I can accept that. I'm not trying to force you to believe anything, I'm just telling you the events from my perspective.

Avery: Thank you for being receptive to what I have to say. I don't wish for you to not be able to say anything about what I'm telling you. You have every right to your own opinions and thoughts. I want you to know that I do not simply see our mother as being an evil person. People are thoroughly complex. I remember the good as well as the bad. I suppose that unlike you, the bad things I experienced with our mother outweighed the good for me.

Blair: There is something I have to tell you, whether you believe it or not: our mother did not give you up willingly. When you ran away, she called the cops to report you as a runaway to try to bring you home. I was there for that conversation, and he cautioned her not to try to drag you back home. He said that in his experience, if you try to force a kid to come back, they tend to run away again. And that the next time, she may not know where you were. That at least you were somewhere safe and not on the streets. He convinced her by scaring her that you could be put in more danger. Whatever else you may think about her: NEVER doubt that she wanted you home with us. Getting that call that a warrant was being placed for her arrest for Child Abandonment…I still have no idea where those people got that idea. And even with all of that, we were still hopeful that you would want to come home. She didn't want to have to drag you back kicking and screaming, she wanted it to be your choice.

Avery: I know that she called the police and I know that the details of that conversation probably happened. I don't doubt that at all. To me, nothing looms quite as large as that day in the courtroom. You said our mother wanted it to be my choice?

I believe that, but I was a child. I feel that it's important that you understand that I wasn't just a runaway teen. I was literally drowning because of the pain I had endured with her and what she allowed to happen to me. Again, I don't want you to think that I am trying to vilify her, but the decisions that she made did not only affect her. It affected me in the most personal and painful ways.

Blair: Who was it that hurt you? You say that she allowed to happen, what do you mean by that? What pain did you endure with her? I never saw a hint of abuse, our mother adored us more than anything. I don't understand.

Avery: This is the incident that was too painful for me to talk about via text. It's the catalyst for everything that followed. I don't expect you to understand automatically, but we did have two different mothers.

Blair: I'm pretty sure I know what you're going to say, and trust me: I get it. I was nine when it happened to me. I was nineteen when it happened again. And I was twenty-two when a guy decided "No" didn't apply to him. I get not wanting to talk about it, but I don't understand why texting is the issue. Do you think I'm going to use it against you? Try

to hurt you with it? I mean, I know you don't really
know me anymore and that makes it hard to trust.
I'm just trying to understand.

Avery: Was it Lance?

Blair: No, the fifteen year old boy who lived next to me
when I lived with Dad. She met Lance
after that, I believe.

Avery: There aren't words that are good enough to
express how sorry I am that that happened
to you. I don't think you would use
anything against me, I'm simply saying
that it's my experience and I need to
communicate it in a way that feels more comfortable for
me.

Blair: I've been sitting on two decades worth of what-ifs
and pain, and I'm just trying to understand why it
all happened. You say we had two different
mothers, but you haven't said how she
was different with you than me. I never saw
a hint of abuse with her. I mean, this is the
same woman that cried when she had to ground
us. I'm trying to compare your experience
with mine, but I have no frame of reference
for her exhibiting that kind of behavior. When a parent
abuses one of their children and then that child
leaves, the abuse doesn't stop, it just transfers to
a different target.

49

Avery: I don't know where you are getting your information from, and frankly it doesn't matter. Our mother never cried when she punished me. I never said she abused me physically. The fact remains that she dragged us all across Georgia, from man to man. Most of them, if not all, were incredibly abusive (verbally or physically), and she certainly didn't do a damn thing about it when I told her about Lance. You may believe the best in our mother, and that's your choice, but what I saw was a woman who couldn't put her children first and get herself out of the cycle of abuse for them. The same woman who told me for years that your father and mine were the same person until I had to find out from your father that it wasn't true. The same woman who told me all of my life that my middle name was Nicole and I found out when I left (finally getting a hold of my birth certificate) that Nicole isn't my middle name. The same woman who couldn't bother to tell me that our grandfather had died. I had to call our aunt to find that out. He was the most important man in the world to me. You have a right to feel how you do about her, but I also have a right as well to my own experiences. The things that she did you may have not seen, or they may not have even bothered you if you did. That's fine. But they bothered me. They hurt me.

Blair: How old were you when you found out we had different fathers? What is your middle name, if not Nicole?

Avery: 10. It happened when we were staying in Douglasville with a man and his daughter. I can't remember their names. After that, our mother told me about my father and I had one phone call with him while we were living with Lance. I never heard from him after that until Farrah found him when I was sixteen. He was not worth finding. My middle name is ████████. After a great grandmother. I have my birth certificate and my original SS card. They both have ████████. Nicole doesn't exist.

Blair: Mama never hid your name, though. I've known Your name is Avery Nicole ████████████ as long as I've known my own. Okay, so your birth certificate doesn't say Nicole, but don't they only let you put one middle name on it? She probably just prioritized the one meant to honor some relative, and left it off in everyday life, cause you always hated it. You said it was a stupid, old-fashioned name.

Avery: They let you put as many names as you want on

a birth certificate. Even when I was born that was the case. There are people I've known who are around my age that have multiple names.

I knew you wouldn't understand everything. That you couldn't understand everything. You didn't want to understand everything. Our conversation served only to reinforce our own notions of our mother.
I knew then I might have to let you go.
I cried.

Confession

The year you turned sixteen I wrote your name in my note-book one hundred times. Sixteen times for each year of your life and eighty-four times for each moment I wished I'd said

I love you. goodbye.

PART III:

THE SURROGATE

(Age: 15)

Avery leaned forward on the oaken bench where she was sitting, straining to see out of the window on the opposite wall. She watched the distant shapes of people transform and shift as they walked by the courthouse in which she was awaiting her fate. It was the only courthouse in Dandridge, and its belly was decorated entirely with relics of the civil war: guns, tin-type photographs, medals, and letters from former soldiers and governors that were protected within large, glass cases. Under normal circumstances, she would be pressing her face against the glass, pouring over everything those cases contained, consumed by curiosity for lives lived so long ago. Today, however, she found herself consumed instead with scrutinizing the faces of the men outside – those who were passing by and even those walking up the steps of the courthouse to enter the doors. Every jawline, every wrinkle, every low-light in their hair was subject to her discerning eye.

It was only after a few moments of this frustrating exercise she asked herself who it was she was looking for.

Her *real* father. Her mother. A parent who wanted her.

"It shouldn't be too much longer," Farrah said as she squeezed Avery's hand.

Avery looked down at their joined hands. They were nothing alike. It was obvious to anyone with sight that they were not related by blood. Her own hands were pale, slender, and still bore the scars of the childhood fights with her sister. Farrah's hands were aged and heavily freckled from years of sun damage. A few heavy, gold rings polished to perfection wrapped around her fingers and were stark contrast to the severely chipped black nail polish she wore. Avery realized then that her hand had gone numb from Farrah's grip. She squeezed Farrah's hand and lightly pulled her own out of her grasp.

Farrah asked her, "Are you going to be okay?"

Avery could only nod. A few minutes passed. She heard the clacking of heels somewhere down the hallway of the courthouse, but her gaze never left the window. A few minutes more. The old clock on the wall was ticking the seconds. Outside, it began to rain, driving those walking by to the general store across the street. A flash of blue-green eyes caught her attention. She rose. He was coming up the stairs of the courthouse. She made her way to the window.

Looking him over, she was mystified. His dark blue sensible suit, his close-cropped, light brown hair, strong jaw and sure gait made the hair on her body stand on end. *It could be him.* He reached the door, and she tore herself away from her perch at the window so she could watch him come inside the courthouse. Avery's heart raced and pounded so hard she thought it was like to burst as the door finally opened. As his figure emerged in the doorway, his eyes turned and met hers. She froze, unsure of what to say or what to do.

No spark, no recognition emanated from his stare. He turned away from her, quickly disappearing down the hallway, leaving little pieces of her hopes in his wake. She felt her shoulders slump down, heavy under the weight of her disappointment. Avery did not look at Farrah, who she was sure had witnessed the entire scene. She did not want her comfort; she was quite used to performing that task by herself. She heard the clock again, each tick bringing her fate closer.

It was then that she thought of her mother. Even though the wounds her mother caused her were still open and fresh, she wanted her mother to show up today. Avery wanted her to show up and tell her that she still wanted to be her mother. That she was not willing to let Avery be taken away. She wasn't sure why. Avery was still bleeding inwardly and took great pains to ensure no one was aware of how serious her condition truly was since she had come to stay with her boyfriend Matt and his mother, Farrah.

I will have a new mother now.

"I would give her to you if I could only keep the $500 her father sends me a month for child support."

Remembering the words of her mother only deepened her wounds. Unfortunately, Avery had been collecting similar phrases and actions from her mother her entire life. She stored them behind a wall in her mind, hoping to never experience them again. But she had also learned that the wall only served to stem the flow of the memories. It never stopped them completely.

The doors to the main courtroom opened. Several people shuffled out of the doorway, their faces sunken and solemn. Avery wondered if her face would bear the same expression once her own verdict was reached. She heard Farrah rummaging through her bedazzled, blue suede purse. Avery chuckled inwardly.

The word 'eccentric' must have been invented for a woman such as her. Farrah's fried, frizzy blonde hair shot out in all directions from her face as if in a desperate attempt to escape her scalp. Her eyes were a shocking crystal blue, the result of color-contacts, but Avery preferred her natural green eyes. Farrah always insisted on wearing bright pink lipstick, which more often than not, ended up on her teeth and building up in the corners of her mouth. Her clothing was bedazzled too, from her shirt all the way down to her four-inch black clogs. Apparently, the fashion of the nineties was her constant inspiration.

After a few more minutes of searching, she pulled a packet of crackers out of her purse.

Farrah looked up, realizing that Avery had been watching her, and asked, "Are you hungry? I'm starving. Maybe this won't take too long, and then we can go down the street to Tinsley-Bible and get some burgers. Want some crackers?"

Avery shook her head. For her, hunger had not yet arrived. Her entire body it seemed was intensely focused on the tasks at hand: waiting and searching. Back outside of the window, cars were rolling by, slowly making their way on the one road which ran through the town. She returned to her project, waiting for the sudden impact of recognition as she watched the men in the parking lot. The clock ticked again. Eight fifty-five. Five more minutes. Fate was approaching fast. She felt the onset of nausea as she surrendered herself to what she was too terrified to admit earlier: *no one is coming for me.*

Farrah rose and walked over to her. She grabbed her hand, squeezing harder this time.

"It's time to go in." She looked out of the window with Avery for a moment, allowing her to have a little more time, knowing she didn't want to move. Then she said, "I don't think they're coming."

Farrah didn't say anything else. She didn't need to. Avery moved away from the window and walked into the courtroom, hand in hand with Farrah. Once inside, she looked around. It was nearly empty, save for four other people. Their tired expressions suggested they had been waiting for quite some time. The judge called a name, and it didn't belong to them, it belonged to her. She took one last look toward the door, tears heavy in her eyes, praying that one of them would walk through it. At this point, it didn't matter which person it was, she only wanted someone to come through the doorway, someone to fight for her. Someone to come in and say, "You're mine and I want to keep you." But no one did.

Farrah put her hand on Avery's shoulder, nudging her forward to the small podium at the front of the courtroom. Now she knew her fate. The judge never had to tell her. She would be given to Farrah and a new life would begin. Now, she would always be Avery the Orphan, Avery the Unwanted. Looking at Farrah, she knew that she wasn't entirely unwanted, but it could never be the same. She was still only a child. A child who wanted her parents.

The verdict passed.

Confession

I never wanted to be a part of your family. You made it only too easy for me to find comfort and happiness in myself. But I lied to survive, to get out, to look for my exit.

Would you care to know why?

It was apparent

It became clear

A swift reversal of attitude

You took charge of a fifteen-year old girl who had just run away from her mother, her sister, from the familiar abuse and neglect and terror.

She came to you broken, suffering from wounds you had neither experienced nor could understand yourself, and instead of accepting her imperfectness, *you berated her for not meeting your expectations and destroyed her when she could not fit so well into the mold of your family.*

you'rejustlikeyourmotheryou'rejustlikeyourmotheryou'rejust-likeyourmother*LIAR*you'rejustlikeyourmotheryou'rejus-tlikeyourmother*LIARLIARLIARYOU'REJUS-TLIKEYOURMOTHERYOU'REJUST-LIKEYOURMOTHER*

Did it feel good? Did it feel cathartic for you to label me what you should have called yourself? After all, I did see so much of my mother in you.

MAN TO MAN. ABUSE AND NEGLECT. SELFISHNESS.

YOU FUCKING HYPOCRITE. You made me more broken. So I left you like I left her, but this time it didn't take me fifteen years. And I didn't even leave a note.

(Age: 26)

In your own words:

04/23/2013, 11:24 PM

"I want a relationship with my daughter-I always have wanted you since the day I felt your bio Mom didnt…I have NEVER EVER lied to you or represented anything but the truth! I could go on & on-you too I am sure-about whose at fault here. HOWEVER, at this point I am not worried about that. I am writing to you against the judgement of others. I am not worried about that, either. As I said to you the last time we spoke-when you said your other family told you I received more money than the $500 your dad sent me eventually for child support and the small amt. of money your Mother gave me and was $5,000 behind that I never received-I am here for you and that hasn't ever waivered. I told you then as I still tell you now-I do love you and always have…if you want to speak to me, day or night, my number is ███████████. I love you…and my grandchild too (I just found out about) ♥ Momma"

(Age: 19-20)

Revelations: The Third

We were crammed into a one-room suite, the six of us.

Mostly made up of your family,

two boys that weren't.

We were crammed together into a one-room suite to survive.

You, being a slave to your sleepy illness and Adderall and vodka, still felt yourself above menial work, so it fell to myself and the two newcomers to support the whole.

It wasn't long before they dropped out of the workforce, so I was alone in my

endeavor for the survival of the six.

I made my health suffer, working without breaks at a Chinese restaurant. The new boys along with your son dreamed of a business online. Your young daughter was helpless. You were drowning in your vodka.

All I asked for was enough money to go see a movie. Only once. You refused and all at once I saw everything. Everything that I had been so stupid not to notice before.

Vodka was not a necessity.

Handing over my entire paycheck to you in support of six people, who,

except one, were all capable of either helping or of supporting themselves,

but instead relied on a twenty-year
old girl who'd left college because

she was told her *family needed her.*

It was time to leave. I'm an expert at leaving. I
couldn't justify sacrificing all that I had thrown away for
this *family* that would never be mine but would certainly
use me as they could.

*I got out. I lived on a friend's couch and cooked and
cleaned in lieu of paying rent or utilities. I got my driver's
license. I bought my first car. I moved into my own apart-
ment. I have never looked back.*

PART IV:

THE FATHER

(Age: 10, 7)

The beginning was the ringing of a telephone. It was sitting on an end table like any other end table, in a room like any other room, in a house like any other house, in a town like every other town Avery had ever lived in throughout her short life so far. The ringing telephone was an unassuming color, somewhere between beige and cream, and it was no extraordinary model. Like others of its time, it was leashed to the wall, and the cord which connected the receiver to the base, lay in a tangled mess of ringlets which no one ever bothered to fix. The volume of its ring was permanently stuck on a note just above the one used by those singers who frequently shattered glass. So, whenever it began its irritating song, it was never long before someone in the house answered it. After all, they really couldn't afford to replace the windows.

Avery never could understand it: she had her mother's cheekbones, smile, and the same almond-shaped eyes, though she shared nothing with him. Each day when her "father" would arrive home from his long days at the recycling plant where he worked, he would fall onto the plush, maroon recliner that he claimed for his own some years ago and shift his body until he was satisfied that he was in the most comfortable position possible. When this was done, the little blonde Avery would climb into his lap and insist that he listen to all of the adventures she had that day. He was always patient, absorbing every word, while his fingers absentmindedly moved over the blue and yellow paint stains on the left arm of his chair.

Avery was the one to answer the telephone today. Her mother was in the kitchen cleaning the dishes from lunch, and her sister had once again disappeared into her own bedroom.

"Hello?" Avery asked into the orange-shaped receiver.

"Avery, is that you?" A question for a question. It was a familiar and welcome voice.

"Daddy! Are you coming this week–"

"I'm not your Daddy. Let me speak to your mother."

The stains were her accidental masterpiece. A few months earlier, she became overwhelmed by a desire to create a great work of art for her "father". Avery could think of no better gift than to paint a beautiful picture for him on the chair he loved so much. She possessed no paints of her own, so she decided to borrow some from her mother's craft room.

Exhilarated by her plans, Avery quickly set herself to the task at hand. She opened the jars of paint, and the smell of the acrylics made her feel triumphant. She dipped her fingers into the yellow paint, then the blue, and pressed them onto the chair making small swirls right along the edge of the armrest. She soon lost herself in her work. There was no time, no space, no dimensions at all, only the masterpiece.

ImnotyourDaddyImnotyourDaddyImnotyourDaddyIm-notyourDaddyImnotyourDaddy

It was upon her then. Reality came upon her and was able to penetrate this barrier of delusion and naivety that she kept just above the surface of her skin since she was old enough to really notice things. Once Reality was in, He set about destroying the barrier utterly, which took about seven seconds exactly. Just enough time for her to put the telephone down on the end table and call for her mother who was still in the kitchen washing dishes. When her figure appeared in the doorway between the kitchen and the living room, Avery pointed to the telephone.

"AVERY NICOLE, WHAT ARE YOU DOING?!" Her mother's voice broke pierced the boundary of her concentration and she became aware again.

She could not remember the lecture, but she remembered the discipline. However, Avery could remember nothing more clearly than her "father's" reaction when he arrived home that evening. He barely made it through the doorway when her mother confronted him, informing her "father" of her crimes of stealing her paints and of ruining his favorite chair. Her "father" looked at the little girl, her right hand covered in blue and yellow paint, a terrified expression on her face, and then to his chair, once maroon and perfect, now splattered on the left armrest with swirls of colors.

"It's for you, it's – it's D–" Avery couldn't finish. The words felt like a brick that she was trying to push through her keyhole-sized mouth.

Her mother, however, didn't seem to notice Avery's difficulty Imnotyour Daddy. It was no great matter, she never noticed much anyway. ImnotyourDaddyImnotyour-DaddyImnotyourDaddyImnotyourDaddyImnotyour-Daddy

Her mother called her into the kitchen Imnotyour-Daddy. It wasn't clear to Avery how long she had been there since the telephone first rang.

Avery's "father" looked at her and smiled, saying, "You know what? I like it better this way."

The little girl's entire body swelled with pride and she felt as if she and her work were validated.

A few weeks later, Avery sat with her "father" in his maroon, blue, and yellow chair, she began recounting the events of the day to him, telling him that her teacher, Mrs. Belliveau, was educating the class about genetic traits.

"Mrs. Belliveau said that we get our faces from our mommies and daddies. I have mommy's smile, see?" She produced a very large smile, showing every tooth in her

mouth.

Avery's *"father"* looked at her and smiled back lovingly, saying, *"You sure do, sweetheart. That is definitely your mommy's smile."*

His gaze returned to the television set they kept on the opposite wall.

Avery's mind was bursting with information about genetic traits. Her attention was drawn to her *"father's"* arm where it was resting, covering her paint swirls. She held up her arm next to his and noticed his dark skin which was lightly freckled and incredibly hairy. Her own was small, pale, and was severely lacking in the freckle department.

She was undeterred. Avery continued in her endeavor, her gaze now fixed on his face. She knew her eyes belonged to her mother, her smile, and her cheekbones. What belonged to him? She studied him for a moment, scrutinizing every detail which was left to her to compare: his eyebrows were much too thick and of a completely different hue – a chestnut brown, the same as his hair, and much too dark for her. His ears were more rounded than hers and made their home much closer to his cheekbones than hers did. Even his nose, clover-shaped, was a polar opposite of her small button-shaped nose. Her sister owned an exact replica of his nose, though. She felt her own nose and grimaced. *'Whose nose is this?'*

Avery walked into the kitchen and sat down at the table, her chair and her body turned toward her mother's back.

"He said–"

"I know what he told you, Avery." Her mother said, more aggravated than comforting. Her back still faced Avery.

"I don't understand." That was all she could manage to get out.

Her back still faced Avery, as if mocking her.

Howcouldyouyourenotsupposedtolieyouremymother- whywhylookatmeyouowemelookatme LOOK AT ME

An eternity passed between them. Questions invaded every corner of her mind and their whispers became roars and then she realized her mother had spoken again.

"It wasn't for you. It was meant for me. He loves you, you know that. It was meant for me."

"Who is he?"

"He-he…well, he left us, Avery. The day you were born. He was married and he left us at the hospital when you were born. He doesn't matter."

Hedoesntmatterhedoesntmatterhedoesntmatter

Revelations: The Fourth

I have often thought about you, FATHER. Probably more than I should have, though I certainly do not feel as if I have wasted any of my time doing so. I was always in pursuit of answers, answers which you so cruelly denied me. But I have reached my own conclusions based on my observations since we first met.

Did you think I wasn't *listening*?

Did you believe I might not be *watching*?

Allow me to teach you what I have learned:

Whether you were married, separated, or divorced when you and my mother began your relationship makes no matter to me. Whether you knew or were not aware of my existence at my birth makes no difference to me now as it did not then.

I was ten when I discovered you, for which I do not blame you. I heard your voice for the first time when I was twelve. You made promises then, that one day that we had together, connected by a telephone. You were gone after that. What happened to cause you to disappear does not matter to me. I hold no anger with you for that, I felt you might be as scared as I was, or else that my mother ran you off.

What do I say now?

I didn't give up on you, but inevitably, I couldn't hold my focus on you as my mother insisted on tossing me around in her bedlam. I lived, but not well, and I still thought of you from time to time. I cannot say that I held myself together with *fantasies* of the two of us meeting, and you then carrying me off to this new, rose-colored world. I have lived *too long* to allow myself such hopeless wishes. *I knew I would meet you, though, and I did at fifteen.*

That moment, brought about by the surrogate whore, I still consider one of the sweetest moments of my life. However, it has also been the source of my despair and confusion regarding your words and actions thereafter.

But, seeing you, god, it's so hard to perfectly describe without making it sound sugary and ridiculous. *Oh, well. All of my wounds were sewn up and healed without scars in one instant.* I forgot the enormity of the pain I had carried for so many years and was made new when I saw your eyes. My eyes. My nose. My smile. It's absolutely cliché to tell you that I was complete, finally, but there it is.

Do you even remember the promises you made then? I do. They were fast promises, and smelled highly of falseness, but I was too happy to take my instincts seriously.

You paid for my airfare. I met grandparents, cousins, aunts, uncles, cats, and lizards. I saw you maybe three or four times that summer. So desperate was I to *belong*, to please you, that I did something I can never take back. You were gone again, but this time not silently. *You said you never promised anything or said that this would work out. You must realize what a terrible lie that was.*

You allowed me to hope and you destroyed it; you

destroyed what was left of *the child*. This is what I blame you for. If a relationship or even contact with me was not what you wanted, you only needed to say so at the start. I've dealt with far worse. But you obliterated something *precious* in me that I can never reclaim.

Maybe you don't feel as if you've missed anything *worthwhile, but you have.*

(Age: 16)

Confession

Choosing a religious denomination is one of the most important decisions of a person's life.

I chose Catholic. You were a Baptist.

I wanted your love and acceptance so desperately that I marched willingly into that church of yours and was baptized in your faith. A moment that only happens once.

I never heard from you again.

PART V:

THE SELF

Introspection or Narcissism? Call it whichever you prefer…

It's been a messy life.

> *How do you begin to sift through a lifetime of stories?*

Someone was once called "cousin"

> *How do you question begin to question everything you've been told?*

then "aunt" then "not blood."

> *My story is also my mother's.*

But they can't be nothing

> *The same grandparents who made my life magical*

if they always were someone

> *destroyed my mother's innocence when she was much too young.*

to me,

> *It can't be true, Right?*

Right?

> *Who can I believe? Who is the villain(s)?*

Each member of a family

> *Was my mother's mind warped long before I was born?*

against one another.

> *A child who never had a chance to*

begin with?

One cries "abuse!"

> *I guess so, depending on who you*
> *believe. Who do I believe?*

while the other says "it's fine."

> *Was there not some bit of humanity*
> *left in the soft tissue of her body?*

Did she love me?

> *Or was she really evil all*

the way   *through?*

Who do I believe?   *Who can I believe?*

I built a wall, a wall, a wall, a wall.
Everything behind it could destroy me.
Everything behind it will destroy me
one day.
I built a wall, a wall, a wall, a wall.
Everything behind it I put there.
Everything behind it needs to stay there
always.
I built a wall, a wall, a wall, a wall.
I'll keep plugging up the holes
so nothing leaks through.
So no one can see me/you.
I built a wall, a wall, a wall, a wall.
Everything behind it could destroy me.
Everything behind it will destroy me
one day.
I built a wall, a wall, a wall, a wall.
Please don't hammer it down.

(Age: 19)

Confession

Death by apple seeds.

That is was all they would write in my epitaph.
You want your exit to be memorable, right?

They would find some irony in mine. The **"survivor"**, the
"strong" girl would take

                herself out with pureed cyanide.

Bleach burns, knives are messy, guns are too quick.

                All commonplace. Ho-hum.

*Death by apple seeds. That was all they would write in
my epitaph.*

(Age: 13-14)

Once upon a time, a young girl named Avery fell in love with the stars. Each night when she was certain that her mother and sister were asleep, she would quietly slip out of her bed, tiptoe through the house while listening intently for any signs of life, and then rush out of the front door of the house.

Each night the stars welcomed her. At her arrival, they shined and sparkled; for a time thereafter, the girl herself shined and sparkled. She climbed into the great oak tree that made its home right outside of her bedroom window. Branch by branch, she brought herself closer to her true family.

While she climbed, the heavens sent soft breezes that lovingly played with her small, white cotton night-gown which was spotted with bright-green frogs. The rough bark of the great oak felt soft to the little girl's bare feet. To her, it was a more celebrated sensation than the silk sheets her mother purchased for her the week before, insisting they would ward her against her restless nights.

Her mother could never understand. For Avery, the nights were alive with magic. When she finally reached her favorite branch, the one which cradled her spine in such a perfect way and allowed her head to rest gazing upward, she was able to see the Universe. Gazing at the vastness of those small points of light, she began to feel connected to something more ancient than herself. This was a home. A home for orphaned souls throughout the eons. It was calling to her soul, always calling.

For a moment she closed her eyes and listened. She heard. She heard its mysterious calls to her in all possible languages. It croaked to her in the guttural language known only to the bullfrogs. It sang to her wispy lyrics in the wind's tongue. She heard it in the quick movements of the rabbits in the nearby bushes.

The little girl decided that she must finally answer.

Avery opened her mouth and whispered to the heavens, "My orphaned soul is yours. I wish to come and live among my true brothers and sisters."

Her body felt lighter, and her pain eased as her soul retreated from her body and made its escape to join its brethren. The little girl watched as it flew above her, climbing higher and higher as she had always climbed her beloved great oak each night. At last, her body rested.

She awoke the next morning in the harsh glare of the summer sun. The perfume of the night air had long faded away, and the melodious sounds of the night were replaced by the angry buzzing of bees nearby. She shifted on the branch, but the bark was no longer as soft as she remembered. It cracked and flaked under her weight, falling to the ground as earthen snowflakes. As she climbed down, an emptiness gripped her.

The little girl ran into the house, afraid that her soul was lost forever. Avery had not expected to awaken in her body, but among the stars instead. She believed that her body would have shifted with her absence, eventually becoming a part of the great oak tree. She felt condemned, and everything that usually granted her smiles was suddenly failing to produce happiness within her. Even Avery's favorite foods were as ash in her mouth.

She became desperate to regain her soul, or to find a way to join it in the heavens. The little girl went into her room and searched her bookshelf for any material on astronomy. She was looking for one in particular that contained star charts. When her hands finally came upon that holy text, she never let it out of her sight. It became to Avery another limb – one that was critical to her survival. The little girl felt certain that her soul had found a home somewhere between Venus and the constellation Sagittarius. Studying the charts tirelessly, she copied what she could onto a sheet of paper, knowing that by using this map to the stars she would find her soul.

Night arrived, and Avery rushed out her front door to greet it, prepared for her expedition. The little girl climbed the great oak once more, bringing herself to that same branch where her soul fled from her. She pulled the folded map from the small, front pocket of her nightgown, and began her search. Glancing from the star map to the sky, she matched the points of light to those on the paper. She then spotted Venus, at last, and then steered her gaze to the left, seeking the one that would be shining with the familiar light of her soul.

The only emotion that filled her hollow shell in the past week had been her desperation. She was surviving, no longer living, crying out to either join her soul in the vast expanse of the night or to have it returned to her. Without it, she was afraid of the years to come.

And then suddenly, there it was! Her brilliant, blue-white light shined right in the middle of Venus and the constellation Sagittarius, just as she'd expected.

Avery quickly tucked the map into the pocket of her nightgown and set out to reclaim her soul. There on her favorite branch, she laid her head against the trunk once again, her eyes never straying from its light. She called out to it, commanding it to return to her body. The star never moved. Her soul refused to return. So, she waited. She waited for the familiar ceremony of the night to begin.

The little girl thought that maybe it was during this sacred ceremony that her soul would return just as it had left. She waited for the frogs to speak, but they were silent. She craned her neck to try to hear the song of the wind, but the air was still. She looked to the bushes and waited to hear the rabbits at play, but the bushes were as stone.

Avery knew it then. She knew it. The night was the Piper and it played its music and lured away her soul to some distant land. A land so happy that her soul would never return to her keeping. She cried. She cried and cried and cried until she was certain she would set upon the earth another Great Flood. She did not think she could continue to live separately from her soul, to endure this utter emptiness that filled her skin since it left her. Her tears persisted, falling upon the bark of the great oak.

The bark began to shift beneath her. It moved swiftly and came upon her skin as a swarm of locusts, seeking to overcome her entirely. The Earth, the Darkness desired her, to swallow her up and fertilize itself with her sadness. The little girl felt a moment of fear, but that moment was quickly destroyed by an onslaught of vicious apathy. She let the bark cover her, and little by little the Swarm gobbled up her legs, stomach, and then her arms. As a member of the Swarm reached her soaked cheek, she looked up at the star for the final time.

It twinkled. A sound mixed with relief, happiness, and surprise escaped her mouth just as the bark came upon her lips. She cried out.

In the bushes, the rabbits began to play.

Revelations: The Fifth

Happiness is the Stranger.

I believe I was familiar with Him in my
childhood.

And perhaps it was that I abused His gifts and demanded
so much of His time that he departed from me without so
much as a goodbye letter.

Throughout the years He has slipped in and out of my
life, quick and sneaky as the *fox.*

And because I had been so bereft of His presence, I too
often failed to recognize Him (He was constantly changing
His hairstyle) before again He was gone from me.

Perhaps then it is better that we remain
separate, for that fear is far more terrifying than
my lifelong companion: Sorrow.

Sorrow and I have in fact, now exchanged our vows
and rings of Union. We apologize for not posting invites,
but we figured it'd be a rather dreary event.

You see, my husband cannot stand the sight
of food, is quite averse to the daylight, and fine
lace causes Him to itch.

Happiness was always the flight risk. I could never have
made Him my husband.

Sorrow is faithful and is always

home by six every night.

PART IV:

THE BROTHER

(Age: 32)

Revelations: The Sixth

The ground has fallen out from under my feet.

Apparently, it was never really there to begin with. I hurt.

I am hurting.

I have no other way to say this, but nothing in my family

is as it seems.

Everything I have known is not as it seems. I've lost my

sense of steadiness

and I am quite positive I am about to fall apart. Liquify or

break into a

thousand devastated pieces.

Brother(s). Is there only one, or three, or two?

To be honest, I have no fucking clue.

        In the course of a several phone calls and

a few days. I have brother(s).

(Age: 32)

Confession

"It was so good to talk to you. Really happy we were able to link up and talk! Means a lot that you are willing to talk to me! Almost brought me to tears to be honest. Love you. Even though I haven't met you I love you. Still my family."

Fucking Christ. I have a brother, maybe more. But, right now I have *a brother*. A brother who loves me. A brother who is my family. A brother who wants to reach out as greedily as I wish to embrace him.

A familial tether within me is strengthening, born from my blood

vessels and molecules. Your voice awakened it. Your words fortified it.

I have a brother. A brother who looks exactly like our mother.

I don't plan on letting you go. I won't let you go.

In the End...

There was a house. A house on a hill overlooking a church. A house on a hill with willow trees planted just for her. A house on a hill with a wooden swing made just for her. A grey house on a hill overlooking a church. It was grey on the outside, *was it grey on the inside too?* but not on the inside. Inside was magic, *was inside destruction? was inside pain?*. Inside was love, *was it was it was it?*.

The inside was occupied by furniture, none of which matched. The inside was occupied by hard carpet and strange floors that weren't level. The inside was occupied by people, *were they really monsters?*.

Family*(?)*.

Her family*(?)*.

A little girl, her grandmother, her grandfather, and her aunt. ~~Family. Magic, and love, and family~~. At one time the little girl's mother was there with them, but she had gone away, *was the abuse she endured in that house gone away with her?*. She was with a husband and another little girl. Her sister, they called her. The little girl often wondered why her family wasn't her mother and her new husband and her new little girl. But being with her family at the grey house on the hill overlooking the church with the willow trees planted just for her and a wooden swing made just for her was perfect*(?)*.

Anytime she remembered it as she grew up, she would think of climbing into the sink to watch her aunt outside from the window. She would throw bread over the fence in the backyard for the birds. Then she would come back inside and the two would watch as the birds flew in. They would try to name each kind. *Was the kindness she gave so freely to me denied to my mother?*

She would remember the age of her grandfather's hands. He called her "precious jewel" and "sugarplum". *The voice that was so sweet to me was silent for my mother. Is that true? Is it all true?* She would remember her grandmother searching for her all over the house when they played hide-and-seek. She would remember it all bathed in the yellow and orange hues of sunset.

It would end. The little girl named Avery would have to leave this place of magic, and love, and family *and the sweet illusions of ignorance*. Her mother would come for her. It would be the only time in Avery's life that she came for her.

There was a grey house on the hill overlooking the church with willow trees planted just for her and a wooden swing made just for her, and ~~she never saw it again~~ *its image wove itself into my sinew and muscle in the form of a question mark*.

The truth, the truth.
Nothing is beautiful except the truth.
Your truth,
my truth.
Let there be nothing else but that.
Should I give you only half,
or do I owe you the whole
of all the genuine
little pieces of my soul?
Would you know me any better
if you knew it all?
If you got a better look
beyond the wall?
I think not.
It's not all I've got.
I'm more than the lot
of these 14,121 words.

The Garden of the
Golden Children

Advisory

This story contains mature themes, including child abuse, that some readers may find unsettling.

Reader discretion is advised.

A MAP OF SOMEWHERE

Somewhere-Else

Somewhere

The Garden

The Academy

The Council House

For those who have endured, part 2.

"They held me and told me everything would be fine, that sadness would rise from our bones and evaporate in sunlight the way morning fog burned off the river in summer. My mother rubbed the kites on my hands and arms and told me to think of my lungs as balloons.

'I just want to feel safe, I said.'"

-Shane Jones, *Light Boxes*

1.

(Just because)

We all live somewhere.

And indeed, theirs must have been the best Some-where, because they always referred to the others outside their borders as Somewhere Else. When the people of Somewhere spoke of the shadowy places beyond their own territory, they did so with a gesture above their heads that looked as if they were clearing the air of dust.

But Somewhere was never spoken of without an emphatic capital S, so the people knew that theirs must be special.

The Academy

The astonishingly white marble was succumbing to an invading army of ivy. Many windows on the lower floor were barely visible, and those on the second floor were mere inches away from the crawling vines. The people of Somewhere were desperate to be rid of it, and each day a unit of the community would take turns removing the green intruder, tearing away at the ivy until the Academy was once again pristine at dusk.

But such was the determination of the plant to swallow the structure, that it returned each night while the people slept, creeping across the marble at such an alarming rate that they felt they were doomed to repeat the process of removing the ivy until the last human grew brittle with age and died.

Then, at last, would it triumph.

A small minority of Somewhere were certain it was

an ill omen, for the ivy had appeared at the Academy following the arrival of the new Headmaster and the disappearances of eight children.

But the majority said that was superstitious nonsense.

Plants behaved like plants.

And the Headmaster was a gift.

It never occurred to the people before his arrival to litter the landscape of the Academy with roses. Those flowers were grown exclusively by the gravemaids, who used them to adorn burial mounds and bodies. As such, when some saw the Academy grounds, they felt as if they were standing in a gravesite. But the Headmaster chided the people for this custom, telling them that beautiful things did not belong to the dead.

It also never occurred to them to send children to Somewhere Else for what the Headmaster touted as an "elite education." And over the course of his tenure, he selected eight children whom he believed exceptional, and therefore would benefit from higher learning in the mahogany hallways of the academies of Somewhere Else.

"The knowledge they will learn will be a benefit to Somewhere," he told the Council while his slender fingers with knotty knuckles curled over the shoulders of the first boy who would depart for Somewhere Else.

"This will benefit Somewhere," echoed the Council to the people.

"This will benefit Somewhere," the people told one another with hopeful expressions.

The children had yet to return and Somewhere had yet to benefit.

Soon after the first boy left, there appeared a life-sized golden statue of him in the great Garden of the Academy. Then another of a young girl sometime later.

Then another.

Then another.

Then another, until there were eight golden statues in the Garden.

Sons and daughters offered to the foreign winds in
pursuit of knowledge to benefit Somewhere.

Thoughts on time, the first.

Time is a hell of a thing. It shuffles everything along, willing or not, toward ruin with absolute indifference.

I once wrote a list of things Time has taken from me when I was much younger, but as so often happens, it was also lost to Time, that ever-reaping force.

Or I might have lost it somewhere in the mess in my room I haven't yet bothered to clean.

Ellis spent an inordinate amount of time wishing she didn't have to attend the Academy.

She hated the roses.

They reminded her of her grandmother—an owlish soul in an ancient body with hands scored by deep valleys between the mountain ranges of her arteries and veins who spent her life tending to the dead along with the other gravemaids.

Her grandmother was magic. Magical. A supernatural being whose sweetness was unmatched by anything the world had to offer, who brought Ellis wide smiles and the soft yellows of sunshine to color her childhood.

When she died, she took all of those things with her, and Ellis spent the following years burrowing so far into herself that her skeleton and muscles and organs and gristle became something resembling her own burial mound—miles of dirt and darkness between her and the light above.

Still, the roses of the Academy loomed large over her, watching her as she said goodbye to her parents at the broad red door to the school, their suffocating gazes serving only as a reminder of what was lost.

That crushing sensation continued into the hallways of

the Academy, which were so thoroughly clogged with students clad in their uniforms that Ellis was certain she would be lost in a sea of red and gray fabric. Then a familiar hand shot through parallel towers of teen-aged boys and ripped Ellis between them like a fisher-man reeling in his catch.

A tight hug. Arms that she knew better than her own.

Kal.

"I am so glad I found you. I have been looking for you for twenty minutes!" He pulled back and studied Ellis with his seafoam gaze.

Ellis threw her hand up between them. "I know, Kal, this uniform doesn't suit me. I really wish it weren't red."

He took hold of Ellis' hand and the pair moved with the crowd, which had begun its march toward the amphitheater. "It doesn't look so bad, but I think blue would suit you better."

"Any other color would be better than red. I feel like I belong with my grandmother and the other grave-maids wearing this."

Kal examined Ellis more seriously as they approached

the amphitheater that was situated next to the Garden. His hand loosened its grip on hers. "My parents aren't too happy either with the changes the new Headmaster made to the Academy, but I have to attend. What would I do without the training I need to work with medicines?"

"I know," was the best answer Ellis could come up with.

He smiled and used his free hand to smooth out the collar of her vest. "Come on, let's go find a seat."

Kal weaved the two of them through the crowd of idly chattering students to an open spot near the edge of the amphitheater. Patches of moss married the stone of the structure and was cool to the touch when they sat down next to each other.

Kal remained close to Ellis. He was always close to her, and she never minded. It had been like that since the two were little. Kal was like a part of Ellis. Her body. Not like a limb, mind you. Limbs can be lost and are hopelessly expendable. You could learn to live without an arm or a leg, but Ellis could not say the same about Kal. He was her ribcage—a network of solid bones encircling everything of hers that needed protection.

He was her best friend.

"Did your parents cry when they were leaving?" Kal asked as he plucked small handfuls of spongy moss while they waited for the assembly to begin.

With each handful he uprooted, the heavy smell of soil in the atmosphere between the pair increased.

"They did. Mom more than Dad."

More earth. More pillowy moss.

"Wish mine had acted normal enough to cry. All they did was sniff at the roses and complain about the air being damp or something."

Ellis pressed her shoulder against his. "You can't really blame them, though. Most of the parents have been complaining about the roses for a while now."

Kal let some moss fall onto the gray and red pants of his Academy uniform. "But the Headmaster has the backing of the Council. I wish they would just let it go. What would we do without the Academy?"

"I don't think it's the Academy they want to get rid of."

He gave Ellis a severe look. "Well, they are the ones who put him in that position, aren't they? The parents adored him, even though they knew he was strange. They knew he came from Somewhere Else."

"He *has* done a lot of good for the community."

He brushed the moss away from his knee. "And they know that too. So, either support him or replace him. There must be at least three of the elders on the Council who would love to be in his place."

"The elders are too reclusive for that, but I'm sure a few of the workmen would be happy to." Ellis tucked an errant wisp of black hair behind her ear.

He nodded distantly and turned to face Ellis, startling her. "By the way, there is something I need to talk to you about…"

The amphitheater was suddenly too quiet. Ellis looked up from her feet and spotted a few instructors standing on the circular platform of the stage—a structure also under attack by ivy and moss. She recognized many of them from times long past, when she helped her grandmother prepare the bodies of their relatives for burial. They whispered to each other dressed in linen and worried expressions.

The students followed their movements with interest.

Once the huddle dispersed, only one instructor was left on the stage. His egg-shaped body seemed determined to stretch the limits of his frame. He was well marked by age too. The pipe-like veins of his hands peeked through forests of coarse white hair and his face was peppered with liver spots and wrinkles. All of his features were crushed under the weight of his brow, making him appear more caricature than human.

But there was no Headmaster in sight on the platform behind him.

There were a few annoyed groans from the students.

Everyone wanted to get a look at the man whose designs had altered the shape and purpose of their beloved Somewhere.

A strange wind snaked through the assembly, and it carried everything, along with Ellis' attention, away with it. She was drawn to the Garden, her gaze tracing the shapes of the leaves in the fading sunlight. Kal noticed her distraction and squeezed Ellis' hand, but she was unmoved. There was something. Something there in the Garden. Something the strange wind was slinking toward.

The Garden's presence towered over the rest of the Academy landscape. Roses peered out from the shade of their greenery, silent archivists keeping a thorough record of events, competing with the elders to weave the best account of its history.

But to the raven-haired girl, they only spoke of grave dirt and waxen corpses.

Ellis shuddered.

The blooms danced and darted left and right, pushed in their movements by the teasing wind. And as she watched, the shadows in the Garden moved, converging upon a single form that was motionless between the Garden's path and the roses.

An alien heat formed in the seat of her stomach. It spread quickly throughout Ellis' body, finding no exit.

Someone was there.

Someone was standing still among the roses like an eerie figure in an oil painting.

"Ellis," Kal's throaty whisper punctured the steel of her focus.

Movement.

Their schoolmates stirred, shaking out their numb limbs from idleness, and began making their way to the dining hall. The wind had calmed, and there only remained whispers of it winding through the grass.

Ellis was suddenly drawn to the sensation of her small hand in Kal's larger one. His eyes met hers and he tilted his head in the direction of the dining hall, then took hold of her other hand, lifting her from the ground.

But her mind wasn't with the movements of the students or Kal or herself.

These simple and familiar motions of her body were now odd and not her own.

Everything of hers was with the roses and the shadowy form that had caused such chaos in her body.

Thoughts on life, the first.

Hell if I know.

Students were filing into the dining hall in neat rows of red and gray.

Large lanterns and an enormous domed skylight soaked the dining hall in orange and purple hues. The walls were uncomfortably white, a stark contrast from the beautifully polished wood of the rest of the Academy rooms. Tall, cylindrical columns stretched from floor to ceiling in rows parallel to whitewashed stone tables. The lanterns twisted around the columns, thrusting light in every direction.

No roses.

Ellis couldn't help but notice. It wasn't simply the difference of color or light, but the absence of roses was everywhere she looked in the room, and that absence allowed Ellis to relax for the first time since she had arrived earlier that day. Kal smiled at her, then pointed to a table.

"Kal! Ellie!" shouted Rowan, and Ellis cringed at hearing that nickname that only she used.

"Hey!" Kal called back as they approached, finding a seat near the end of the table.

As soon as Ellis was in her seat, Rowan turned to her and said excitedly, "Can you believe it, Ellis? We've been talking about this place for years now and finally, we are here!"

Ellis returned her smile, but replied flatly, "Yeah."

Rowan frowned and leaned in closer, her honey-colored hair spilling over her shoulders to occupy the space between the pair, and whispered, "What's wrong? I thought you were excited about coming here."

Ellis managed a stealthy glance at another group nearby—all its members chatting enthusiastically about the coming year.

"I'm getting this weird feeling... The roses... I-I can't... It's just all so bizarre."

"You sound like our parents!" She giggled, her chocolate eyes sparkling.

Ellis bit her lip. "I know, I know. I guess I just don't understand why the Headmaster is so willing to put them on display at the school."

"Who knows? I mean, he isn't from here. Maybe it all means something different where he's from?"

It was the well-worn theory on nearly all lips of Somewhere.

Ellis didn't respond. She followed Rowan's gaze across the table to Nox, the fourth member of their group. They were all quite ordinary enough for their ages— clumsy of body and speech, each action never quite in line with intention, and bursting with desires both fleeting and fierce.

A tray of food was placed on the table in front of Ellis, and she glanced up to see one of the kitchen aids retrieving trays from a cart crafted from the same whitewashed stone as the tables. She had a kind face that complemented her small frame, and she was silent as she worked. Not that Ellis could have heard her over Kal's boisterous laughter in response to some inappropriate joke of Rowan's anyway.

The savory scent of heavily spiced, roasted meat provoked a rumbling in the empty cavern of Ellis' stomach. Inhaling deeply, Ellis permitted the rising steam to flood her senses. She caught a note of vinegar and grimaced. On her plate was a large portion of pickled root vegetables. The worst of all vegetables.

Waste was prohibited in Somewhere.

Things were made to weather. To last.

And whatever you were given you accepted without complaint.

Wincing as the potent vinegar washed over her tongue, she did her best not to retch. Kal used his spoon to scoop the lion's share of the vegetables from Ellis' plate and deposited them on his own. He winked at her and then turned his attention back to the group.

The exchange was not missed by Rowan. She leaned in to Ellis, her voice low. "So, have there been any developments with Kal since the start of summer?"

Ellis took another bite of the bitter food, fighting against the biting flavor, and shook her head.

"Well, I'm sure it's only a matter of time—"

"Rowan, Ellis, you two should come with us to the river at week's end. We need to get all the sunshine we can before it gets cold." Nox adjusted his glasses, his dark hair sweeping across their thick rims.

Rowan threw a fist in the air. "You know we will. Right, Ellis?"

Ellis nodded. Her mouth was still full of vinegar and vegetables. She didn't want to speak another word. In the wake of Rowan's questioning, Ellis only wanted to retreat into herself and not emerge again until Somewhere was lost to time.

Ellis' stomach soured as the light of the lanterns grew brighter in protest of the darkening sky, and she couldn't be sure if it was vinegar or nerves.

Kal had wanted to tell her something earlier.

She wasn't sure she was ready to hear what he had to say.

Thoughts on love, the first.

Is love a live thing, like a human or animal or plant? It must be nurtured to thrive. Tended to with sweet words and thoughtful actions.

And it is laughably easy to destroy.

The strike of a fist.

The slow torture of indifference.

Betrayal.

All only wounds.

But wounds heal eventually. Tissue regenerates and muscles too often remember their use. And so, there is this question left: if love can perpetually heal, can it ever die? If it cannot die, then it cannot be a live

123

thing, for death is the fate of all live things.

What is love, if not a live thing?

It must be something above live things.

Some greater force akin to gravity or the wind, which we humans experience and borrow on and employ when useful. But like all greater forces, it will outlast us and carry the impressions we've made on its surface throughout the infinite.

What a comfort that is.

In every corner of the building, students were preparing enthusiastically for tomorrow. For the lessons, for their futures. But Ellis' room was still as a tomb. Beams of moonlight shone through her window, illuminating the room in a soft glow.

She removed her uniform and set it on the dresser for tomorrow and retrieved a cotton shift from the middle drawer. The thin material hugged Ellis' skin welcomingly. She opened the window to the night air and the scent of roses greeted her. It was shut quickly in frustration and the teenager climbed into bed, wrapping the sheets around her.

Nebulous time passed.

There was no settling. No sleeping.

Restless limbs and an equally restless mind.

Then, a light tapping on the door.

At first, Ellis was certain she had imagined it. But it continued and became more insistent.

She stumbled out of bed, her breathing a bit choppy.

Tiptoeing toward the door, Ellis kept telling herself it would go away, and that there wouldn't be anyone on the other side when she opened it.

Her hand grasped the knob and she steadied herself, inhaling so deeply that she became slightly dizzy.

When Ellis finally opened the door, she was met with a pair of eyes the color of seafoam.

To the wild-haired girl

in the front...

In the Great Library of the Academy there rested a forgotten epic squeezed in between two volumes detailing the agricultural history of Somewhere. It was plucked from its place one day by a librarian's assistant who noticed it wasn't shelved correctly. He put it on top of the unsteady stack of books that was already struggling against gravity to remain atop the cart and wheeled it along the rows of shelves to the front desk.

When he swerved to avoid a student rounding a shelf, the epic fell to the floor where it was promptly snatched up by a girl with apple-skin curls who determined that she and the book were meant to meet and checked it out at the front desk.

She was walking back to her room holding the epic tightly against her chest when fingers much too thin to be normal curled over her shoulders and led her into a dim office.

Ellis rubbed her eyes in disbelief. "Kal? Are you all right?"

"Can I come in?"

"O-of course." Ellis stepped aside to allow Kal to enter and then shut the door. "Kal, what—"

His arms were around Ellis in the space of a second. She could hear the hammering of his heart through bone and skin. He kissed the crown of her head and whispered, "I know what Rowan asked you, but know this: I will never push you, Ellis. Ever."

Ellis' body relaxed against his. She never really expected anything less of Kal but couldn't stem the swell of relief she felt at his words.

Kal's embrace loosened and he stepped away from her, reaching for the door. "I just couldn't go to sleep without telling you." His smile was warm. Ellis returned it. "Will you come to the river this weekend?"

"With everyone?"

"Yeah. Nox suggested it, remember? Thinks it will be a good way to end the first week."

"Sure."

Kal opened the door and before he shut it, he glanced at Ellis and smiled once more. "Night."

"Goodnight, Kal."

The soft click of the latch sliding into place came with another wave of relief.

Nothing was happening.

Nothing would happen.

Thoughts on time, the second.

Where does the past go to live? Is it carried solely in the memories of all species only to be destroyed piece by piece as Death visits, or is there some wondrous place in the universe where the past has made a home?

Discoveries made over and over again.

Wars on an endless loop.

The sweetest moments replayed and never vanishing.

Some pocket of the universe where everything lasts.

A place where I can snuggle into the arms of my grandmother and never let go.

The classroom was wholly unlike the rest of the school. Remarkably lifelike roses were carved into the walls. It seemed there was no escape from them. But the rich, dark wood was absent, and in its place was some sort of gray stone.

Gray desks in neat rows.

Gray writing board.

Gray-haired instructor with gray eyes.

Time was a slippery thing as the students shuffled into the room and to their desks clad in their red and gray uniforms.

Slip.

Slip.

Chitter and chatter. Laughing faces. Nervous faces. Familiar faces.

Faces still as the gray stone of the room.

A cough.

The squeak of a chair leg as it was moved.

Slip.

Slip.

A bright bloom of red curls appeared in the doorway framing the tiniest girl Ellis had ever seen. Blue-green eyes and a generous smattering of freckles across the equator of her face. She was a brazen riot of red in the gray and gloom of the schoolroom.

She couldn't possibly be real.

She was a character from some story who breezed inside and all at once, there was color.

Knights had slain great beasts for her hand.

Poets had written endless lines in meter detailing every constellation in the freckles on her cheeks.

The Fates had tracked her destiny since the birth of all

things.

And Ellis could not take her eyes off her.

Her gaze traced the curves of each curl as the girl chose an empty desk at the front of the room, lost in the labyrinth of red, until she spotted a red and gold chocolate wrapper embedded in a section in the back.

Without thinking, Ellis tore a small scrap of paper from her notebook and hastily scribbled something and sent it up the rows without ever really looking away from the girl and the chocolate wrapper.

Ellis watched with the eagerness of a puppy as the girl unfolded the note and read it. She reached into her hair and located the chocolate wrapper with such ease that Ellis wondered if she had already known it was there. Then she wrote something on the scrap of paper and folded it around a tiny object that Ellis couldn't quite make out because the girl's arm was blocking her view.

Ellis counted her heartbeats until the note was passed

to her.

Thirty-eight.

To the wild-haired girl at the front—

You have a chocolate wrapper in your hair and I really want to be your friend.

Hello, New Friend!

My hair catches everything except luck it seems. But thank you for letting me know!

-Ofelia

Inside the note was a chocolate in a red and gold wrapper.

Ellis smiled so wide that she was certain the corners of her mouth touched her ears.

She put the chocolate and the note in her jacket pocket.

Somewhere in the atmosphere of the room, or maybe it was in the atmosphere of her soft tissue and sinew, something shifted.

The aged hands of the elders worked nimbly at the Council House, spurring ink across pages long stripped of their original words. The mothers of Somewhere found employment at large looms, weaving records of time's passing into delicate, complex tapestries, the groans of the willow wood echoing through the dusty hallways.

The last group of the Council cleared away the skeletons of relics with weathered hands, pulling apart the threads of frayed tapestries and the pages of dissolving tomes as deftly as they extracted roots from the fields or crafted elegant shapes from stone or wood in the making of each of Somewhere's structures. These Council workmen offered the pieces too marred by the constant assaults of Time to the fire, a fitting sacrifice for Death, the universe's great devourer. What they could save became components in new archives, connecting the span of years together, continuing the Council members' dance in the shadows between the forces of Time and Death, striving to keep their little pocket of Somewhere protected and hidden.

But still they knew that none could hide forever.

The Headmaster

"Are you going to spend breakfast in a daze, Ellis, or are you going to sit and eat something?"

.

.

.

"*Well*, Ellis? Hello?"

"Huh?"

Nox pointed to a free seat at the table next to Rowan. His bright eyes and thick lashes made his expression appear less severe, even though Ellis knew that wasn't the case.

Rowan patted the seat and smirked. "Yeah, Ellie, come sit by me and you can tell me all about how things are going between you and Kal."

Nox gave Rowan a withering glare.

Ellis was dying inside.

"You know you want to hear about it as much as I do."
Rowan scoffed then pouted, her thin lips struggling
to achieve the full effect, but quickly abandoned her
cause. "Scoot down, Nox. I want Ellie to sit by me." Her
honey-colored hair was in a tight bun and made the
sharp angles of her face stand out more than usual.
She looked like an instructor rather than a student.

"Where's Kal?" Ellis asked as she sat.

Nox was the one to answer. "I knocked on his door this
morning, but he never said anything. I assumed he was
with you."

Ellis blanched at his remark but had no response to
give. Instead, she took a bite of the heavily buttered
bread Rowan offered her, hoping they would soon find
something else to talk about.

"There he is!" Rowan shouted. She thrust her hand in
the air. "Kal, over here!"

Thank goodness.

Kal's trademark goofy grin was on full display. He
jogged over to the table, and Ellis noticed that his
uniform was a bit mussed. Probably just woke up.

"Rowan, could you sit with Nox? I want to sit next to

Ellis," he asked, his grin still plastered on his face.

As he dropped into the seat Rowan vacated, his heady scent filled the air between them. He took her hand and squeezed it, and in an instant, Ellis was calm.

The kitchen aids soon brought food for Ellis and Kal—a simple bone broth, boiled eggs, and summer berries, the last of the season. Ellis smiled. The berries provided some much-needed sweetness and color to the intensely white dining room.

"Kal, where were you? I thought we were going to walk together this morning?" Nox asked between steady puffs across the hot broth on his spoon.

Kal, in the middle of sipping water, gulped quickly and replied, "Sorry, I was held up."

"Held up?" Nox glanced up at Kal, his glasses falling forward on his long nose.

"Yeah, I ran into the Headmaster early this morning when I decided to go for a run in the Garden."

Suddenly, summer berries didn't seem as interesting.

Suddenly, all of the air in the room had evaporated.

"You met the Headmaster? What is he like? Was

he nice? Oh, I heard he's cute! Is he cute?" Rowan wiggled in her seat excitedly, but her high bun remained a steady rock upon her head.

Kal couldn't suppress his laughter at her enthusiasm. "He was actually pretty nice." He took a bite of an egg after sprinkling it with a bit of pepper.

"You cannot leave it at that! What did you talk about?"

"Rowan, let Kal eat before you jump all over him," Nox chided.

"Mind your own business!" Rowan glared at him for a moment, then returned her attention to Kal. "Please, tell me! I've been dying to meet him since we arrived."

Another bite of egg.

He grimaced this time.

Too much pepper.

"It wasn't anything special. He asked about my family, my friends…if I was enjoying lessons. Pretty normal stuff."

Ellis' nerve endings broke away from their main system

and squirmed through her muscle like worms in wet soil as conversation about the Headmaster continued.

Her stomach was like the stone of the dining tables as the syllables of his title rolled from their tongues.

Then the berries turned sour like vinegar.

Thoughts on life, the second.

Sometimes I see life events like waves breaking upon the rocks of a shore. Each one can bring with it good or bad or both, and the rocks would never know which until the water crashed against them.

Nutrients.

Organisms looking for a home.

Millions of particles of salt.

Crushing force.

Whether good or bad or both, the waves devoured the rocks, bit by bit, until there was nothing left. All would be lost to the sea. Events devoured a person in much the same way—whether good or bad or both, they lured the minutes of a life from a body until there were none left.

Some events capture more minutes than others, and I have this sinking feeling that a large portion of minutes are about to be taken from me.

Ellis hugged herself and counted to one hundred.

Nothing was going to happen.

Nothing is going to happen.

The hills and forests that dominated the horizon on all sides of Somewhere were multiplying and rising in the distance. It was the workmen toiling in the outlying lands who first noticed the phenomenon, worrying that the ground beneath their feet was collapsing while the borders swelled. Initially, they thought they were suffering some delusion brought on by the abnormal heatwave so late in the season, but the next week the trees and hills stood taller, and the ground had retreated further downward.

The workmen called for the elders to inspect the changes to the borders, their colleagues on the Council, who were equally anxious about the changes to their territory. They were certain that the ascending hills and forests on boundaries of Somewhere was another omen, like that of the ivy swallowing the Academy.

The Council members grumbled their concerns into their cups of wine at sunset, watching the landscape around their beloved Somewhere change.

An excerpt from A Treatise on the Excellence of Somewhere, written by an elder from the eighty-fourth year after the founding of Somewhere.

…for indeed, so fortunate is Somewhere in its geographic position, that no overly inclement weather ever visits. It is surrounded on all sides by forested hilltops, protecting the country from invaders and an oversaturation of outside influence, which would be a detriment to our people and the propagation of our way of life.

(23) In the center of this circle of greenery, is Somewhere proper, a place of good society and jubilant spirits who live their lives in service to this nation, sharing labors and yields, having no dreams of grandeur other than the legacy of Somewhere. Contribution is the livelihood of the people—a duty instilled in them from infancy. And though societal roles are not assigned, it is nevertheless expected of each person to devote themselves in roles that will uplift and benefit their country. This has made the people of Somewhere happy. Not a forced or untrue happiness, but a pure and absolute happiness.

(24) And how could they not be so? Their homes are made of sturdy stone set in the purest white, each with its own necessary facilities and small garden. The

people see to their own needs and care for the needs of others, so that none are hungry or cold. But the shining jewel remains the Academy—a place where the youth of Somewhere are educated and trained to fill their roles and see to it that our land and our ways live on in perpetuity.

(c) It is here that this author will make the conclusion that Somewhere can rightly lay claim to achieving Utopia, illustrated by the evidence preceding this passage and the thorough examination of the withering lands of Somewhere Else in sections 7-17. There can be no doubt that a life in Somewhere is much preferred and desirable than one Somewhere Else, and that this Utopia will thrive so long as its citizens are dedicated to its health and the security of its future, preventing us from coming under the direct gazes of Time and Death, who seek the destruction of all things.

The river zigzagged around the Academy grounds, and in the haze of the afternoon it would be a welcome respite. The friends approached the soft mud of the riverbank and quickly discovered they were not alone—many other students were already swimming in the cool waters, enjoying the last bout of warm weather before autumn arrived.

Rowan marched ahead, saying, "Well, we aren't going to get any cooler standing here staring at everyone."

Nox and Kal smiled, and then all followed in Rowan's wake. Ellis was already uneasy about being seen in a swimsuit. Not enough fabric to hide in.

They found an unoccupied spot in the shade of a large oak tree. Its thick branches twisted out in every direction toward the sky as if they were trying to escape the trunk. Some of the leaves were marked by patches of orange, yet another sign of the fading summer.

Skin was freed from the scratchy cotton of the Academy uniforms. Ellis' heart thundered between her lungs, and Rowan's eyes widened as she caught sight of her plain swimsuit. She said nothing.

Cool water against hot skin.

In the lazy current of the river, the children of Somewhere played.

Kal's laughter echoed across the surface of the water.
He and Rowan were chatting with some students of
another year downstream. Nox swam laps from bank
to bank, constantly weaving around the throngs as they
splashed and giggled.

Ellis took a breath and disappeared under the water.
It was blessedly quiet. In the cool murk she could only
rely on touch. Tomorrow, she would have to endure
the frenzy of activities and lessons, but today there
was peace. As she rose to the river's surface to take a
breath, hands as familiar to her as her own snaked
around her waist.

She turned, and her black eyes met his seafoam ones.

His warm cinnamon skin was even darker in the sun,
and Ellis watched as droplets of river water cut paths
down his collarbone and chest.

Rowan shoved Kal forward. "Don't be shy!"

The pair's bodies collided, and Ellis shivered as flesh
met flesh. And while her body fit perfectly against his,

the shivering increased at such an alarming rate that she was sure she would retch. Ellis pulled away from Kal and swam to the riverbank. Forgetting to grab her uniform, she sprinted away from the water and her friends and straight to the safety of isolation. And it was isolation that brought her to the entrance of the Garden.

Drenched and with muddy feet.

The bile rose, turbulent and quick, and Ellis vomited into the rose hedges.

"Are you all right?"

Ellis froze. It was a voice unknown to her, with a buttery tone that would cause most to swoon at the sound. She wiped her mouth with her wrist. "I-I'm fine. Thank you."

She couldn't bring herself to look up.

A red handkerchief gripped by slender fingers appeared in her line of sight. "Here, use this. Please."

Ellis looked at the embroidered cloth—beautifully sewn roses—and shook her head. "I'm fine. I need to get back to my room."

"Can you get there by yourself? I could help."

There was something burrowing around in her liver, something scratching and screeching. She needed to get to her room. She needed to get to her room.

"Ellis?" Kal approached and his fingers threaded through Ellis' hair, sweeping it back from her face. "I'm here. It's okay."

"Ellis. That's a lovely name." It didn't sound so lovely in that buttery tone.

"Headmaster, thank you for your help. I was worried Ellis wasn't feeling well."

"Oh, it's no trouble at all. I was just enjoying a walk in the Garden and spotted her. She wants to go to her room. Would you mind taking her, Kal?"

"Of course. Thank you again."

Kal let go of Ellis' hair and she finally found the resolve she needed to stand upright with him beside her.

Dark eyes.

Dark hair that fell haphazardly around the Headmaster's face, the ends kissing his stubbly jawline.

Tall, thin frame.

He was disturbingly beautiful.

She was unable to move.

"There you are. I see the face is just as lovely as the name. I hope you feel better, Ellis."

Something about the way he said her name made Ellis want to cover her ears and never hear another sound again.

She said nothing. She did nothing.

"I've got you, Ellis." Kal squeezed her hand and then crouched in front of her.

She muttered something nondescript and climbed onto his back, her muddy feet sweeping against his legs. Kal waved to the Headmaster and carried Ellis away.

Away. Away.

She buried her face into the nape of his neck, breathing in his scent as deeply as she could, and let him carry her away, all the while swearing to herself that she'd never eat butter again.

Totems

Eight golden statues in the Garden of the Academy representing eight, very real children.

Eight children who had yet to return.

Eight faces cast in gold. Their expressions stoic. Lifeless.

At their feet, an item belonging to them:

A stuffed unicorn.

A journal with a frayed spine and edges.

A bright purple dress.

Two game pieces.

A pair of wiry glasses.

Two sets of Academy shoes.

Ellis wondered what her item would be were she

chosen and sent off to Somewhere Else and cast in gold.
She shook.

She hugged herself and counted to one hundred.

Nothing was going to happen.

Nothing is going to happen.

2.

(this shouldn't be happening,)

A crack in the glass

An icy autumn wind whipped through the open window of a silent room. It skated across an empty bed with sheets marked by starbursts and bounced off the far wall where it met a desk that hadn't been tidied in some time. An old epic lay open there, snuggled between piles of red and gold chocolate wrappers, waiting for its renter to return to the world within its yellowed pages. But it was the fickle autumn wind who visited, turning the pages of the neglected text and scattering several of the chocolate wrappers before darting back out the window into the gray sky, barely taking notice of the shivering girl with apple-skin curls lying on the floor with her knees to her face. But this was no surprise to any who know the autumn wind, for it rarely wastes much time in one spot. It is far too busy seeking its adventures to pay attention when it really matters.

Thoughts on love, the second.

Trapped behind a cage of bones and squished between two oversized, bean-shaped organs is the heart. The engine pumps life steadily throughout the body, relentless in its endeavor. Stories and holidays and parents say it is the seat of love, and so its image has been scrawled in journals, carved into trees, and replicated in art for a portion of human history. And though now we know better thanks to the clever minds who have worked out how human emotions are formed and processed in the brain, we continue to believe in the myth.

Is it because it has so pervaded our society that we cannot wrest it from its place, or could it be for convenience's sake, or perhaps it stems from a more romantical desire to keep the heart on its throne as the place of love since books with lines like, "I love you with all my brain," fall hopelessly short of the impact it needs?

Maybe there is another reason altogether, one which comes from experience. You see, while the clever minds have astounding evidence that love comes from the brain, it is not the brain that skips when you fall in love, and it is not the brain that aches when you're heartbroken.

It has always been the heart.

Extraordinary things often happen on the most ordinary of days. And it was on one such ordinary day in the middle of November that the Council elders stormed the Academy with the cutthroat determination of a conquering army with its sights set on what its generals believed to be a tiny nation ripe for the taking without incurring casualties in their ranks. Garbed in billowy, white robes and their heads framed by equally long, white hair, the elders of the Council seemed more like chess pieces moving across the board of the Academy grounds to checkmate the dark king sequestered in his dim office while the mothers and workmen who served on the Council awaited news of their victory on the soft grass outside.

Not a word was uttered among the students and instructors. The air was even absent the soft trilling of larks that usually congregated in the Garden. The whole of Somewhere froze in time. Some held their breath.

Ellis hugged herself and counted to one hundred.

Nothing was going to happen.

Nothing is going to happen.

Among the uniformed students, a bloom of red curls fell across the rigid shoulders of Ofelia. Ellis' gaze traced the path of each loop from end to root, failing to notice for a moment that the girl was staring unblinking at a spot on the wall at the front of the room. Ellis fought the instinct to go over to her, for though they had accepted one another as friend in name, in truth they were still strangers.

Ellis invented scenarios in her mind of how they might happen upon one another outside of lessons and forge a friendship as masterfully as a smith crafts a weapon. Every gesture and remark carefully designed to bring the pair closer, something Ellis wanted desperately. Ofelia was sunshine in a human body. However, no number of imagined circumstances, though artfully authored, succeeded in bringing the girls together. Ellis knew she would actually have to do something, and that thought terrified her more than the buttery voice of the Headmaster.

The gray-eyed instructor with silvery hair and a grim mouth determined that the students had sat in silence long enough and walked out into the hallway to investigate. The clicking of her thin heels on the hardwood floors faded after a few moments, and they were once again caught in the stifling atmosphere of quiet. Ellis wasn't sure how much time had passed since the arrival of the Council. But judging from the outbreak of fidgeting in the other students, it had been at least twenty minutes.

"Look!" said a boy sitting in one of the center desks, pointing a finger at the large window that faced the town.

The students turned their heads in unison and watched as the Council left the Academy, huddled together and whispering to each other. Defeated. Whatever the cause of the duel, the Headmaster's winning shot seemed to strip them of their convictions. Murmured rumors spread from person to person, varying from plausible to outright outlandish. Ellis didn't partici-pate. She had no knowledge to offer. Her attention was surrendered to the tiny girl at the front of the room who remained motionless, still looking at a spot on the wall as if it were the only thing that existed.

The Headmaster's Story according to the mothers of Somewhere, who told this to their children and children's children, who weren't ready for the sour truth of things.

An adventurer.

Philanthropist.

He emerged from the great river of Somewhere draped in cloth of gold.

The sun shining at his back.

He opened his arms wide and gave to Somewhere everything he had.

Before there was anything, Time and Death sat together in the Nothing. The cosmic twins of destruction felt their purpose beat within them as staunchly as a heart beats within a human. But there wasn't anything to eradicate in the blackness, and so the siblings resigned themselves to the ruin they were meant to wreak.

Time's unmatched skill in decay rusted with disuse, his masterful fingers could no longer coax seconds, minutes, or hours without anything upon which to practice. And without anything to devour, Death's great mouth could no longer open, so her belly sang its solemn song in the black.

Time whispered to Death, "I won't let the Nothing take us. It is nothing, and we are something."

Death only nodded.

Time formed his slender fingers into fists and with every last ounce of effort, pounded them together knuckle to knuckle. When his fists came apart, swirls of stardust spilled into the space of the Nothing. There was light. There was color. There was life.

And life was meant to be destroyed and devoured.

Time stretched his fingers and pried open the great

mouth of his sister, and then went to work pulling seconds, minutes, and hours out of all things. He offered them up Death, who gobbled life in one large gulp and thought she'd never tasted anything sweeter.

Billions and billions of years. All passed. All reaped by Time and fed to Death—brother caring for sister, meticulous and devoted in his labor. We all surrender to this show of love, and we all end up in Death's great belly.

Excitement. Curiosity. Stomach-churning anxiety.

These emotions shifted and raged in Ellis as she stared at the ivy-covered structure the morning of her arrival at the Academy.

There were roses everywhere.

"You're going to trip over your own feet if you don't pay attention, Ellis," her mother said, biting into the red lipstick on her bottom lip.

Ellis said nothing in reply. She pulled at the over-starched collar of her shirt and continued on the Academy path.

"Are you all right, darling? Nervous is normal, you know, especially on your first day. It's such a special—"

"Talking about it isn't helping."

"Okay, okay. I understand. Let's just get you inside and settled." She smoothed an errant blonde strand of hair of hers back into place, then gave Ellis' shoulders a tight, maternal squeeze as they walked together.

The clicking of heels and shuffling of footsteps in more sensible shoes seem to sound in rhythm with Ellis' erratic pulse. There were fathers in perfectly pressed navy suits with golden buttons and mothers in floral

*attire with painted lips. To Ellis, it was a carnival, and
not the sort for children's merriment.*

*"I remember my time here so fondly. I know you'll feel
the same way once you've left. Wonderful experiences
are ahead of you, even with all the changes the Headmaster has made." She frowned at the sight of the roses
carved into the great red door and continued, "He did
revolutionize things, I suppose. Before he arrived, we
knew nothing about Somewhere Else, and now some of
our most gifted children out there, growing in wisdom
so that they might enrich our beloved Somewhere when
they return."*

*"None of them have returned though, have they?" Ellis
said a bit brusquer than she intended.*

*"No, they have not returned yet, Ellis. Do you think that
wisdom is a thing that can be so easily obtained? It
may be many years before we see them return, but rest
assured, they will return to us," she said with convic-
tion, but her expression failed to match it.*

They will return to us.

*It was a mantra, nothing more. Ellis repeated that to
herself each time an adult said the children would
return. Ultimately, she had no reason to reject their
assertion, but she couldn't digest the sensation of a*

167

heavy stone in her stomach whenever the topic was broached.

Ellis said it to herself over and over in the hopes that it would help to lift the rock from her gut. But it hadn't worked, and so Ellis made a mantra for herself.

She sat in her room, hugging herself and counting to one hundred.

Nothing was going to happen.

Nothing is going to happen.

Encounter, the first

There once was a warrior of little standing or heritage living in the wastes of Somewhere Else. Though she had no fortune or title, she was unmatched in battle and fair in her dealings with friend and enemy alike. Her deeds were woven into songs and stories, spreading from town to town across the great continent until there was no place that did not know the warrior's name. And everywhere she would travel the people would say, "She is one of ours."

But there were some who heard these songs and stories and sensed opportunity. To subjugate or destroy the great warrior would raise their own reputations, and so they sought exactly that. Clan lords and middling fighters challenged her in an effort to prove that she was not so skilled as the tales claimed, though each one was offered to Death by her blade. Monarchs and heirs approached her with honeyed tongues and insulting offers to join their harems instead of a place at their sides, which she refused with as much queenly grace as ever was witnessed.

There was one ruler, however, who was unyielding in

his efforts to possess the warrior. Instead of following in the footsteps of his predecessors and proposing paltry deals he knew wouldn't entice, he carved out a place for the warrior as his queen by ridding himself of the current one. She found herself—muscle and bone and vein—changed, a somber, glass figure, placed in the ruler's vast garden of similar glass statues.

And with her timely demise, the ruler had a space ready for his new bride.

Of course, he hadn't prepared for her inevitable refusal.

A slight miscalculation on his part.

So, the warrior was invited to the ruler's palace with the promise of abandoning his designs and hosting a feast in honor of her achievements and their friendship. The warrior was loath to trust the ruler, whose dark gaze and strange, thin hands gave her a sense of foreboding, but she also was hesitant to insult the hospitality of his subjects if the ruler's intentions were true. She knew the only thing to do was to go to the feast with a gracious smile. And she did.

And the people loved her.

She indulged the court in dances and in conversation, telling a captive audience of her adventures in the wastes and beyond. She was patient with idle gossip and petition alike, and when everyone took their places for the feast, they whispered to one another that they would love to serve a queen such as she. They believed they would get their wish too, when the royal guards spirited her out of the room before she'd even managed to swallow her first bite of charred boar.

She had only needed a bit of blunt persuasion.

Glasses were raised to the king and his inevitable queen.

The tower was home to the warrior through a long winter. Each day the king would visit to ask if she would reconsider the generous offer of being queen. After all, the king told her, he could make her eternal, and her name would live on forever. She would be pampered and cared for the rest of her days. She would be free of this tower. Each day she declined, for she knew very well that she would never be free, only transferred from one prison to another. At least in the tower, she was liberated of the expectations of the people and of the advances of the king. But she knew that would not last forever.

Eventually, the king would become impatient, and she worried that she would join the other figures in his glass garden.

There was only one path to true freedom.

When the king arrived the next morning, he found the fierce and fair warrior's body swinging from a make-shift noose of sheets attached to the crossbeam of the tower's ceiling. On her dead face, there was a smile.

And while the kingdom that so desired her to be queen mourned the news of her passing, the king wiped his slate clean, his fingers curling over the shoulders of a new target.

Frost on the ground. Frost on the glass.

A long crack spidered across the windowpane, the only imperfection in an otherwise perfect place. Gray light cast gloom throughout the library, and for a moment, Ellis questioned her decision to come here at all. But when she spotted a familiar red bloom disappearing around the corner of a bookshelf, any lingering doubt vanished.

Ellis tracked the girl's movements in the library, admiring how Ofelia could not seem to help but trace her fingers along the tops of the books, as if she were able to learn everything she needed to know about the stories within by that simple act. She stopped at one that was particularly ancient, with a nearly severed spine and dulled lettering. Eyes wide, Ofelia carefully pulled back the cover and scanned the contents of the first few pages. She smiled.

"Hey, new friend. Have you come to rescue some books as well?"

The question came so abruptly that Ellis wasn't certain that Ofelia had said anything at all until she glanced up from the book expectantly.

"I, um, I'm sorry?"

"The books," Ofelia said as she pointed to the shelf in front of her. "See? So many of them have been waiting for a special person they can tell their stories to. Someone who needs to hear their messages."

"Their messages?"

Ofelia's blue-green eyes sparkled at Ellis' question. "Some of them are pretty straightforward, like in children's stories. But with others you have to really pay attention, or you'll miss them." She closed the book and slid it under her arm so she could continue searching the shelves with a free hand.

Ellis tentatively took a step closer to Ofelia. She had the strange feeling that if she made any quick movements that she would spook the tiny girl, and she'd vanish behind the shelves like a deer into the trees. "How many have you read?"

Ofelia tracked Ellis as she neared, but she didn't move away. "I lost count when I was nine. I used to keep track of them in a notebook, but then I started reading so fast that I sort of forgot to write them down." She giggled and then swiftly covered her mouth, no doubt afraid of being chastised by the head librarian.

"I have a notebook like that, except I write random thoughts in it." As soon as she said it, Ellis wished she hadn't. She worried it made her sound silly. "But it's nothing, really."

Ofelia took hold of Ellis' hands and asked, "You're a writer? I think that's marvelous! I have always wanted to write stories, but I was never any good at writing. I can never translate the stories in my head to paper."

Ellis had no witty reply for Ofelia. Indeed, she did not have a reply of any sort. At that moment, every molecule in her body was only aware of the sensation of Ofelia's hands holding hers. It was nothing like holding Kal's hand, except that there was some measure of comfort that manifested in both. But there was something utterly singular about the feeling Ellis experienced with her hands in Ofelia's—something that was exactly like belonging.

"Hey, new friend." Blue-green eyes met black ones. "I think it might snow tomorrow. If it does, do you want to see it with me?"

Ellis nodded.

Ofelia's wide smile stretched almost all the way across her face. "Let's hope for snow then."

That day when Ellis left the library, she didn't even notice the gray light anymore. The only colors she could see anywhere were blue and green.

Thoughts on life, the third.

How do you begin to measure a life?

Is there a cosmic scale to weigh the value of your atoms, actions, and agonies? And would you be weighed against yourself or weighed against others?

If a person is the vessel of a billion moving parts, can there actually be an accurate formula to determine a person's worth?

In all cases, even the most objective answer is subjective. Everything dependent upon perspective and shaped by experience.

So how do you begin to measure a life?

The hills and forests that dominated the horizon on all sides of Somewhere were still multiplying and rising in the distance. The workmen tracked their height and growing numbers, reporting to their fellow Council members of the changes. The mothers hummed solemnly at their looms while the elders scribbled histories into remade tomes, but the news of their Somewhere's continued transformation struck hard in their hearts.

And when all who comprised the Council came to the center of Somewhere, the ground beneath their feet sunk another several feet, but not so low as the soil upon which the Garden sat. It seemed to them it was the vertex of the change.

They looked at each other in distress, knowing that Time and Death had truly set their sights upon Somewhere at last.

The sun hung low over the horizon as Ellis walked the Academy grounds. The frost still clung to the grass, crunching below her feet. She was headed nowhere in particular, only wanting a chance to breathe the crisp air before heading to her room to study. She looked across the landscape and spotted the roses that littered the Academy grounds. They were dying.

She smiled and hoped it would snow tomorrow.

Momentum and curiosity brought her to the Garden. She wanted to be certain the roses were dying every-where at the Academy. Their menacing presence had worked against Ellis like rust upon metal, eroding parts of her little by little, without remedy or relief. But both came at the sight of rose petals scattered across the frozen grass. With the departure of the roses, the memories of her grandmother sweeping her up and hugging her crept further into the dark corners of Ellis' mind, disappearing almost entirely.

And suddenly, she could breathe again.

Freed, for a time, from the stifling weight of loss.

"Come to see the roses?"

Soft butter on a warm tongue.

Ellis trembled.

A tall, thin frame came into view. "It's quite chilly today. You came without a coat?"

Ellis did not respond. She couldn't even meet his eyeline, but she saw the pale blue of his coat shift as he removed it and placed it on her shoulders with hands that were too inhuman to be human—strange, wiry fingers connected by knuckles that appeared to her like the gnarled, ancient knots of trees.

To any observer, his gesture might have seemed kind. To Ellis, it was like a decisive move by a skilled conqueror.

"Better?"

She managed something akin to a nod and took a breath, a sweet scent filling her nose.

"Walk with me."

Withered rose petals set the course for Ellis and the Headmaster, filling the space between the circular hedges of the Garden. The chill in the air caused Ellis to reach absentmindedly for the lapels of the Head-master's coat, but as soon as she realized what she was doing, she let go. The sweet scent already seemed inescapable, like a vice tightening around her. She certainly didn't want to make it worse.

Somewhat brave enough to look now that his eyes weren't on her, Ellis glanced at him and found herself entranced by the fluidity of the Headmaster's gait. Each movement was a ripple across still water, and Ellis was pulled along in the force of his wake.

They came to a spot in one of the middle circles where a few of the golden statues peeked through the greenery, their expressions fixed everlasting behind a mask of gold. It was there that the Headmaster abruptly turned to face Ellis.

His gaze seized hers.

Ellis' lungs constricted behind her ribcage, squeezing her heart between them so tightly that she was certain this was the moment she would die. There was something cosmic in the power of his gaze, something that made her feel as if she were prey trapped in the celestial fist of some primordial predator.

He smiled, but it was not warm. "Do you like the Garden, Ellis?"

He remembered her name. The sound of those syllables sliding off his tongue made her wish her name were anything else.

The Headmaster's gaze never left hers, but she didn't fail to notice how the wind caught his dark hair, playfully swatting large sections against his stubbly cheekbones. "I love to come here. The forever and the fleeting together in one spot. These golden children remain as the world changes around them. It is something exquisite to watch."

He scanned the unmoving figures of the children and Ellis followed suit. There was something of the eternal in them, but she well knew that Time would eventually steal them as it did everything. The Headmaster took advantage of her distraction and glided across the coiled corpses of roses to her.

Ellis was suddenly aware of every cell in her body.

The unearthly creature stretched out his hand and took hold of the collar of the coat he had lent her, manipulating its edge at the nape of her neck. Ellis inhaled sharply as his thumb traced a trail along her skin and found berth just behind her earlobe. His spindly fingers curled over her shoulder. Her chin trembled. She felt herself—whatever spirit materials she was actually made up of—slide out of the pores of her body.

She was here.

She wasn't here.

She was Ellis.

She wasn't Ellis.

He had overtaken her, and she didn't belong to herself.

As he invaded the space between them, he said to her, "Once I had a sister. A lovely little thing who never uttered a word in her life, but I knew that there was a great fire beneath the calm of her countenance. I cared for her. Oh, I loved her so much, Ellis. I wanted to give her eternity. I wanted her to last."

She didn't understand at all.

She was slipping.

His thumb made small circles behind her ear. "You are so much like her, Ellis. You are quiet, but you are loud inside. I can see it so clearly. Would that I could make you shout, that I could give you permanence."

She slipped, right out of his grasp, hyperventilating wildly.

He didn't move to close the gap between them again.

Instead, he cast her a long look and left her there, shivering and struggling to breathe among the carcasses of hundreds of roses and the frozen faces of the golden children.

It wouldn't snow the next morning.

The irony of touch

Color seeped out of the world as water vanishing down a drain. The ashen landscape was bereft of anything resembling life to Ellis, though its rhythms and melodies were unchanged. The bright cardinals still sang as they worked. Lessons were still as humdrum as ever. Kal was still close in his orbit, still happily caught in Ellis' gravitational pull.

But he noticed the new tilt in her axis, and Ellis was not surprised. Kal sensed changes in her oftentimes before she realized herself. Normally she would let him comfort her—wrap an arm around hers or take her hand—but she shunned his touches for the first time in their lives, drawing more into herself until she, too, almost disappeared like the colors of Somewhere.

And as gray claimed the scenery, it also sought command of her body.

In the patch of skin covering the soft tissue from her neck to the back of her ear, there blossomed cold iron.

Thoughts on time, the third.

All things are eternal borrowers, too many of them fervent in their prayers of thanks to the countless gods who've emerged and evaporated across eons, never imagining that Time and Death are the true gods to which creatures owe their gratitude.

Time is said to sow all things and feeds all things to Death, an endless labor of devotion and care to his sister, whose appetite is never satisfied.

And we, these temporary beasts of the universe, are as miniature replicas of Death's form—our greedy mouths devouring seconds, minutes, and hours as they pass through us, always desperate for more.

Could it then be said that Time is a selfless god?

Is there nothing to be gained from his acts, or are we missing something?

Something important.

Something urgent.

Something we are overlooking with our mouths wide, consuming seconds, minutes, and hours with barely a thought given to the process, outcome, or motive.

Time lent Ellis some of itself.

Three weeks of gray sedation before the red anguish burst through the stagnant gloom.

The people of Somewhere plucked the ivy's ambitious vines from the walls and windows and roof of the Academy. Sweat escaped their bodies as they cleared the structure, but the invading plant was not so lucky this day. It sat in its bundle once it was torn from the marble, scheming and plotting, not at all afraid as the people of Somewhere set it alight. It had innumerable seeds throughout the grounds, and would rise to war again, certain that it would conquer the Academy one day.

It only needed the opportunity.

There was a quiet room in the Academy that belonged to a quiet girl. The room was once kept uncommonly neat, and it, like the girl's appearance, was merely a mask for everything underneath.

But now, the mask was dissolving.

Clothes in various states of freshness marked the landscape from the door to her bed, which was buried under pages ripped from her journal.

Bloodied tissues and washcloths formed small hills on the floor in front of the long mirror where a girl sat using a fresh cloth to scrub the stubborn iron from her neck.

She cried as she labored, her tears spilling into her mouth and souring her stomach like vinegar.

She bled into the clean cloth.

The iron remained.

Tales of Somewhere

Else

Ellis was barely aware of Rowan as she buzzed about the room, sorting clothes and disposing of litter.

Neither said a word.

But Rowan hummed a soft tune, and its melody hung in the air like the heavy perfumes of summer flow-ers. Ellis shifted under her blanket, uncurling herself and stretching her limbs as far as she could reach. Far enough until her joints resisted. She lifted the hem of the blanket and peeked out the window, catching a glimpse of snowfall in a slate sky.

Ofelia was waiting for her, wasn't she?

No, that wasn't right. The sun and moon had set many times, but Ellis couldn't number them. Her days were lately measured in stints of restless hibernation and the chewing away of her fingernails to the quick, not by the indifferent motions of planetary bodies.

"You're awake," Rowan remarked as she tossed some bloodied tissues into a bin by the door. "I've brought some work for your lessons and something to eat from the dining hall. It might be a little cold."

Ellis stared at the covered plate, not feeling anything remotely akin to hunger except for a sense of emptiness spreading underneath her skin like an overturned cup of water across a flat surface. Rowan made to help her friend, but Ellis waved her away and left her bed to fetch the plate herself. She knew Rowan wouldn't leave until she was satisfied that Ellis had eaten and was resting again.

"Kal?" Ellis asked, barely whispering as she sat at the desk and removed the cover from the plate.

"He was here two days ago. Said you were sleeping so deeply he didn't want to disturb you, so he cleaned a bit and left." Rowan took a seat across from Ellis and studied her with a serious expression as the girl pushed cold potato quarters around her plate. "El… C-can I… Do you want to talk?"

The raven-haired girl went rigid, and an oxidized apple slice slid from her fork and fell to the plate without a sound. Rowan's outstretched arm nearly traversed the distance that now separated the two girls, but when her fingers brushed against the curtain of Ellis' raven hair, her shoulder snapped backward, and she shot up from her seat and stood staring at the wall.

Ellis heaved and cried but couldn't speak to her friend.

"Ellis…" Rowan's fingers still reaching for Ellis, she joined her in tears.

Whatever had happened, whatever was happening, Ellis was lost at sea, disappearing into the horizon.

The two friends continued in this way for a time, crying together until Rowan was sure that Ellis hadn't any tears left.

Rowan tucked her back into bed and slipped out the door.

Ellis closed her eyes, and the world sank blessedly into the black nothing as the snow persisted outside her window.

Thoughts on love, the third.

Humans are conquering creatures. They skulk about in the open, determining weaknesses in their quarry. And when they strike, it is to destroy or bring to heel. They plant flags in foreign dirt, believing wholeheartedly that this odd act affords them dominion. They abduct their kin and label them "less than" for reasons that hold as much water as a bucket without a bottom.

Control makes them feel powerful. Control makes them feel as if they are turning the tide against Time's command, even if for a little while.

It is peculiar then that humans should put so much of their focus outward, when a squishy bag that pumps blood squatting in their bodies that influences their lives so heavily is permitted to continue doing so.

Weird creatures indeed.

The epic was discarded and reclaimed many times by the tiny girl with apple-skin curls. She would sneak it back into the library, stealthily avoiding the ever-distrustful gazes of the head librarian and her assistants, and push the epic in between two tedious books on mathematics. Certain that someone would need it. Certain that she didn't need it any longer.

Always a few days would pass, and the tiny girl would return to the library and tiptoe to the mathematics section, believing that anything interesting couldn't happen without some clandestine behavior. The epic was always where she left it, undisturbed and already collecting bits of dust from its neighbors. And so the girl would retrieve it and tuck it under her arm, creeping around the bookshelves and cozy enclaves until at last she would exit the library, victorious once more.

The rhythm of this act was constant in its pace for weeks. The tiny girl with the apple-skin curls smiled to herself and thought she had passed some cosmic test, that the epic and her were indeed truly a match.

But she wanted to be really sure.

She placed the epic in the library one last time and slipped out of sight, planning to collect it again in a few days and then keep it with her forever.

When she came back, the epic was gone. There was a black space in between the two mathematics texts where some dust gathered. The girl left the library and did not return.

In a dim office an epic lay open atop an immaculately polished end table inlaid with perfectly carved roses. A few of its pages were torn out.

The Headmaster's Story according to the work~ men of Somewhere, who kept the account to themselves.

A strange fog hovered over the river that day. Most of the workmen weren't even in the fields yet, but the couriers were already making their rounds despite the weather. A couple of workmen who decided to catch a fish for their breakfast, sat on the riverbank and had barely prepared their bait before they heard it.

A loud sloshing in the river where the current disap~ peared into the bent trees.

The workmen worried that it was some large beast, perhaps a bear. They were about to run when they caught sight of a human figure through the fog. It was a man wearing strange clothing—loose brown trou~ sers and layers of brown shirts. There was a large pack strapped to his back, encircled by a thick rope.

He was dirty. He looked as if he hadn't slept much or slept well in days. But when he spotted the workmen and bits of the town poking through the creeping fog, clinging to his pack with hands that looked like spider's legs, he smiled.

When Ellis opened her eyes, he was lying there next to her. The two weren't touching, for he'd left a few inches of space between them. But he was there, sleeping. The even tempo of his breathing brought Ellis comfort, the first she'd felt since…

Her fingers eased along the warm sheets toward her best friend's sleeping form. She stopped just short of his forearm, suddenly feeling anxiety biting at the spongy lining of her belly. Kal's lashes fluttered. Ellis' heart ached.

A few inches started to feel like a widening gulf, and Ellis feared she couldn't bridge the gap, no matter how close Kal traveled in her direction.

She closed her eyes.

At world's edge in the west, the eight ancient clans of the greenlands celebrated an alliance ending hundreds of years of bloody conflict. Between the two most powerful of the clans there was to be a union—the son of the Evenkii would wed the daughter of the Irtysh. The children of their match would rule the ancient clans, ensuring peace and survival.

The son of the Evenkii was pleased with the pairing, but he was troubled when he learned the daughter of the Irtysh was mute. Whether by choice or act of nature, no one knew, but he longed to hear his bride's voice, so he set out to discover a remedy.

His search brought him to the Old Fen, a marshland near the edge of clan territory populated by black willows carved into human forms and an unusual man with strangely shaped hands who resided in a ramshackle cabin. He was rumored to possess talents that unnerved all who encountered him, but it was his voice which was the most unsettling to the son of the Evenkii.

It was too rich, like over-churned cream.

The man of the Old Fen welcomed him warmly enough and listened to the son of the Evenkii as he spoke of his silent bride. He requested that the son of

Evenkii bring his bride to him, that he might examine her and make his diagnosis. He also requested that
he be permitted to do his work alone, that the son of
Evenkii would not linger while the man of the Old Fen
treated his bride.

Though the son of Evenkii was uncertain about this
request, he ultimately honored it, wanting nothing
more than a solution to his problem.

The daughter of the Irtysh had no sooner bade her
groom farewell than the man of the Old Fen made to
claim her. There was no question of her beauty, but the
shape of her features reminded the man of the Old Fen
of someone he lost in his youth. Someone precious.

He told her fantastical stories of his life and of the
world and of his desire to make someone eternal who
could sit by his side, and when those attempts to court
her favor failed, he determined that he would conquer
her by force. When he came upon her, she trembled,
but still would not speak. Wherever he touched her,
there grew black willow bark. It slithered along her
body until at last, her beauty was captured in the trunk
of a tree.

The man of the Old Fen wept and kissed the rough
cheek of the daughter of the Irtysh and planted her in

the mucky soil. He whispered a secret promise into her petrified ear.

When the son of the Evenkii returned, he found his bride amongst the black willow forest.

The man of the Old Fen had disappeared.

It was during a late afternoon walk when she had a rare moment unsupervised by her concerned friends that Ellis spotted her. Snow gathered in the curls of her hair, which toppled out of the bottom of a charcoal knit cap. Her red-and-gray Academy uniform looked too thin to ward against the cold, but she compensated somewhat with heavy boots and wool stockings. Ellis had opted for something similar, with the added benefit of a thick coat and gloves.

Ellis inhaled sharply, the cold air stinging her lungs, and approached her.

Ofelia's gaze was fixed on one of the statues of the Garden—a boy who couldn't have been more than a year older than the two girls. His frozen face was tilted skyward.

"Where do you think they went?" Ofelia asked, startling Ellis as she neared.

Ellis hugged herself, tucking her gloved hands under her arms. "The Council said they went to Somewhere Else to learn."

Ofelia made a sound that could've been mistaken for a scoff but didn't turn her face away from the statue of the boy. "That's what they say. What do you think they are learning?"

206

"Aren't they learning things to help Somewhere?"

"Are they?" Ofelia glanced at Ellis for a moment, and then returned her gaze to the golden figure.

"What do you mean?"

Ofelia chewed on her bottom lip until a small bead of blood formed in the center. She licked it clean. "Somewhere is Utopia, right? It's written in the books and it's touted by the Council and by the people. I was just wondering why Utopia needed improving, I guess."

"Somewhere isn't Utopia."

"No, it isn't." Ofelia brushed some snow away from her curls. "I wonder if Utopia even exists."

Ellis shifted her weight and tried her best to avoid looking at the statue. The stoic expression of the boy was more than she could bear at the moment. "I think there might be, somewhere out there. Or at least, there's a Somewhere far better than here."

A smile formed on Ofelia's lips, which were cracked from the cold. "You may be right. And I plan to find it."

A sudden surge of sadness rushed through the hollow spaces in Ellis' bones. "You're going to leave?"

"Yes, new friend, I'm going to leave. I don't know when, but it will be soon."

"What about your friends?" Ellis stepped closer. "You'll really leave them behind?"

Ofelia finally turned away from the statue to face Ellis and took her hands in hers as she had that day in the library. Ellis didn't pull away. "I am not afraid of being alone. People were not meant for always. Nothing is."

Ellis shuddered against the wind.

The two girls stood together in the snow in the shadow of a golden statue.

"My name is Ellis, by the way."

Ofelia's smile widened. "Ellis. I've heard that name before in a story I read about Somewhere Else."

"Will you tell it to me?"

"Sure. Hot chocolate first?"

Ellis nodded and the two girls left the Garden and the golden statue behind in the falling snow. Ofelia didn't let go of Ellis' hand, and Ellis still hadn't pulled away.

The ancient air in the Council House was disturbed by fresh threats. The mothers, workmen, and elders whispered to each other of their failed attempt to confront the Headmaster, alarmed by the transformation of their beloved pocket of space in between Time and Death. The elders' tactic had been flawed, the mothers and the workmen agreed. It was time for one amongst their own ranks to have a turn at confronting the Headmaster, for they were certain that Time and Death each had set their own designs on Somewhere, but they were not yet ready to deal with Death.

They would have to settle for contending with Time, as they had in lifetimes before, when they were believed merely to be sages by those who were ignorant of the workings of the Fates.

3.

(it doesn't mean)

Encounter, the second

Time sat by himself at his large desk in the dark, coaxing the minutes out of celestial objects and stuffing them into glass jars marked for Death, who munched happily on her prepared meals and constantly squalled for more. And though Time appreciated the knotty details of his craft, there were times he found himself at his desk wishing that his medium were one of creation instead of destruction. What would such a thing be like that could outlast even him?

He longed for such a thing. Something beautiful and eternal.

Something to sit with him in the long hours of the work.

He passed another jar to his sister, who said nothing, only chewed on a bit of cosmic energy and crawled away to her corner in the dark, content in her solitary feast.

Time sat by himself at his large desk and brushed the glass jars aside to begin his true work.

Resilient winter vegetables swam in a broth that was a bit too thick for her liking, but she brought small spoonfuls to her mouth anyway, grimacing slightly at the bitter aftertaste. She never minded vegetables much before, but lately Ellis had become overly accustomed to sweeter fare, finding little chocolates in red and gold wrappers stuffed under her door each morning or on library shelves in front of books Ofelia was desperate for Ellis to read. But Ellis' pace was much too slow for Ofelia, and so she would often find herself eagerly listening as Ofelia told her tales so masterfully that even ancient storytellers would be envious.

Like the bright flowers pushing through the remnants of the winter snow, Ofelia was bringing color back to Ellis' world.

She still hadn't mentioned Ofelia to her friends.

They still hadn't pried, afraid to tug at the tenuous cords of her deliverance with questions.

But Kal and Rowan altered their courses around her, charting closer paths to protect her from whatever they sensed was amiss which she hadn't yet said aloud. If Nox noticed something horrible had happened to Ellis, he never said a word. He was much like Ellis in that way.

Ellis brought another spoonful of soup to her lips and Kal asked, "You want some apple cake? My mom visited yesterday and left me with a few slices."

His expression was hopeful and warm, and Ellis couldn't refuse him. "Sure."

Her teeth slid into the softened skin of a carrot.

She caught a glimpse of Rowan smiling at the exchange. Ellis knew her friend trusted that things were returning to normal, but she wasn't sure anything could ever be normal again.

She wasn't even sure she knew what normal was anyway.

Ellis swept more hair forward on one side of her neck, hoping to hide the iron stain.

Thoughts on life, the second. An echo.

Sometimes I see life events like waves breaking upon the rocks of a shore. Each one can bring with it good or bad or both, and the rocks would never know which until the water crashed against them.

Nutrients.

Organisms looking for a home.

Millions of particles of salt.

Crushing force.

Whether good or bad or both, the waves devoured the rocks, bit by bit, until there was nothing left. All would be lost to the sea. Events devoured a person in much the same way—whether good or bad or both, they lured the minutes of a life from a body until there were none left.

214

Some events capture more minutes than others, and I have this sinking feeling that a large portion of minutes are about to be taken from me.

His room was messier than she expected, but it was filled with a spicy scent that was undeniably Kal. His seafoam eyes studied her as Ellis scanned the room, taking stock of the unmade bed and numerous discarded sketches cluttering the dark carpet.

She bent to pick up one depicting the landscape behind the Academy. Kal scratched at the back of his head. "I started drawing after the first snow. I've had some extra time since... Well, anyway, I had time. What do you think?"

The shapes were somewhat blurred, and the river was wider than it should be, but Ellis thought it was beautiful. "I like it, but I thought you'd be spending your extra time in the greenhouse? They won't certify you as a healer unless you put in your hours."

"I have been. There's only so much time I can spend there, though."

Ellis was struck by the tinge of melancholy in his tone. "Kal, I—"

His fingers glided across her palm and laced with hers. He squeezed her hand lightly. "If it hurts too much, you don't have to tell me. But I'm here, and I've got you."

Her foundation, already cracked and wobbly, crumbled. Ellis fell into Kal's arms and cried, inhaling the warm cinnamon scent that forever clung to his warm cinnamon skin. His lips brushed against the crown of her head, but she didn't flinch or jerk away. As Kal's arms tightened around her, Ellis swore she could feel the bones in her ribcage strengthen in response, as if Kal were reclaiming his place in the skeletal structure that protected her flimsy insides.

She let Kal hug her a bit longer and counted to one hundred.

Nothing was going to happen.

Nothing is going to happen.

In a dim office, laying atop an ornate end table covered in carved roses, was a suffering epic. A few of its pages were torn out, and in this act it lost something precious.

A little part of itself that no one else might think to miss.

A refrain from the larger plot that was as essential to the epic as cartilage and marrow were to fleshy beasts.

And it had been seized, ripped from the epic like weeds from a garden.

Would anyone ever make it whole again?

Would anyone ever love it incomplete?

It lay atop the end table, its closed cover hugging its remaining pages, the raw wounds buried somewhere deep within.

Starlight swept across the room and over the two figures lying close together on the unmade bed, their arms wrapped around each other tightly. Their steady breathing was the only sound in the room. His fingers sailed through the thin silk of her hair while hers traced the arches of his eyebrows and the angles of his jawline.

Seafoam eyes met black. Neither looked away.

They existed in this new space together, pushing forward inch by inch, careful to mark their path so as not to misstep and tumble.

Kal pressed his forehead against Ellis', the tips of their noses touching.

His fist closed around a large section of her hair behind her head. He gripped it firmly, desperate to not let go.

He held her as she slept, and she dreamed she was a little girl perched in a great tree watching as her soul soared through the night sky.

Thoughts on love, the first. An echo.

Is love a live thing, like a human or animal or plant? It must be nurtured to thrive. Tended to with sweet words and thoughtful actions.

And it is laughably easy to destroy.

The strike of a fist.

The slow torture of indifference.

Betrayal.

All only wounds.

But wounds heal eventually. Tissue regenerates and muscles too often remember their use. And so, there is this question left: if love can perpetually heal, can it ever die? If it cannot die, then it cannot be a live

221

thing, for death is the fate of all live things.

What is love, if not a live thing?

It must be something above live things.

Some greater force akin to gravity or the wind, which we humans experience and borrow on and employ when useful. But like all greater forces, it will outlast us and carry the impressions we've made on its surface throughout the infinite.

What a comfort that is.

Ellis counted her steps in the deserted hallway. The
lights in their glass cages cast long shadows like black
wrinkles on the lavishly adorned body of the floor.
The thick carpet silenced her footsteps, but she wasn't
entirely bereft of sound. A harsh wind thrashed against
the windowpanes. A warning.

A familiar form emerged from a doorway.

A buttery voice called her name.

Her breath caught in her chest, and she hugged
herself. Before she could count to one hundred, slender
fingers curled over her shoulder.

"It's been a while, Ellis," he whispered into her ear. She
didn't respond. She didn't move. "Come with me."

It wasn't a request. The heel of his odd hand propelled
Ellis forward, and the two disappeared into a dim
office. Her throat was a desert, and she was unable to
swallow, unable to get her muscles to obey her in any
manner. He deposited her into a chair next to a small
table populated solely by an old epic.

Ellis stared at an imposing desk, bigger than any she
had seen before and etched with tender scenes between
two humanlike shapes surrounded by nothing in the
dark wood. She heard the lock on the office door click

into place. When he approached her, Ellis braved a glance, and his features softened under her gaze.

The Headmaster kneeled in front of her and brushed aside the black curtain of her hair, baring the patch of iron to his vulture stare. "We have work to do, you and I."

Ellis gripped the sides of her seat so hard her hands went numb and her fingernails cracked.

His dark eyes tracked her tension. "Don't do that, please."

Ellis trembled, and he took one of her arms by her Academy jacket sleeve and brought the palm of her hand to his cheek, directing it over his stubble. As before, Ellis felt herself slipping out of her body, out through her cells and pores. She looked at the ceiling. Tears coasted down the slope of her skin.

"Stay with me. You belong here with me, more than any of the others."

When she didn't look at him, the Headmaster dropped her hand and stood. He went to his desk, his lithe body framed on all sides by walls hidden behind bookshelves stuffed with stories and strange sculptures and empty glass jars. He drew a deep breath and turned back to her and drove his hands through his long, chocolate-colored hair.

Ellis kept her grip on the sides of her chair, certain that if she let go, she would be lost. She opened her mouth to speak.

The Headmaster leaned against the edge of his desk, but it didn't groan under his weight. It was silent. To Ellis it was thunderous. Heavy. Hungry. The silence born of the motives of his movements invaded the tissues of her organs. It was a bile spiraling through her esophagus, gobbling up what remained of Ellis' voice in large measures. It devoured vowels and punctuations, leaving her with nothing to resist his determined gestures except consonants.

"P-p—"

He kneeled in front of her again and laid a hot palm on her leg, his fingers playing with the hem of her red and gray skirt. "You cannot see it, can you? This bright force inside of you that makes you so singular, so special. Its sound is so deafening to me. It reminds me of my sister. She was perfect, beautiful. Just like you. But she didn't last. She couldn't last."

Tears turned to streams, widening as they flooded her face.

He caught her eyes—black to black. "I want you to last, Ellis. You have no idea how much, how long I've watched you, knowing that you were exactly what I needed. Something beautiful and eternal. I can make you last."

Ellis shook and shivered, still gripping the sides of her chair, fearing what was to come. She tasted salt. She heard butter.

The Headmaster's thin and knotted hand coasted under her skirt. "We have work to do, you and I."

Red ruins everything

The son of the Evenkii moved into the abandoned ramshackle cabin and spent his days tending to the black willow form of his bride. He rid her exposed roots of invading plants and encouraged the growth of fungi around her, hoping to ensure her survival while he searched for a way to reverse her condition.

He also searched for any word of the man of the Old Fen, but there wasn't even a whisper.

The man of the Old Fen had simply vanished.

But the son of the Evenkii was of stalwart stock and refused to despair at the difficulty of the task before him. He decided to seek the advice of three sages who lived on the border between the Irtysh and Evenkii territories. The sages were respected for their wisdom, for it was they who promoted negotiations between the Irtysh and the Evenkii, and it was they who suggested the match between the son of the Evenkii and the daughter of the Irtysh.

So he was confident in his choice to consult them.

As he approached the unassuming door to their small home of stone, he was certain the sages would have the answer he needed.

The first sage to greet him when he was welcomed inside was The Lady. Her thick gown was embroidered with intricate flowers, the colors of the threads so bright they shimmered as she glided around the room, which was stuffed to the brim with stacks of books and comfy furniture and oddities from forgotten regions of Somewhere Else. Her striking ruby lips pursed in what appeared to the son of the Evenkii like maternal disapproval when his heavy boots left muddy impressions on a beautiful rug that depicted the sages at work writing and cutting pages from books.

The son of the Evenkii removed his boots and left them by the door.

This gesture seemed to please The Lady, who took the troubled young man by the arm and brought him further into the room where the others sat rifling through books that were so ancient the son of the Evenkii was certain they would fall apart at any moment.

The Laborman greeted him next, smiling at him with thin lips, the tip of a pipe balanced between two rows of yellowed teeth. The Aged greeted the son of the Evenkii last, garbed in the whitest cloth without even the slightest shadow of stain. His silvery hair slipped over his shoulders like water sliding over rock, and with each gesture appeared to move with his body instead of fighting against his motions.

The son of the Evenkii was offered a seat facing the three sages, along with some exceptional wine, warm bread, and spiced preserves, but he hadn't felt hunger or thirst for quite some time. The only desire of his body and soul was of the restoration of the daughter of the Irtysh, his beloved bride. The son of the Even-kii divulged his dilemma to the sages, who listened in earnest to his story.

When he was done, The Lady told the son of the Even-kii that he should pour the purest honey at the base of the daughter of the Irtysh's trunk, for to combat a sour fate required the sweetest tonic. The Laborman disagreed, however, saying that distance was in fact the cure. The son of the Evenkii should depart the Old Fen, giving his bride the space required to emerge from her willowy form of her own accord. Distance, The Labor-man believed, was the tool needed for people to solve their own curses.

The Aged disagreed with both The Lady and The

Laborman. While he believed both ideas had their merits, he argued that they were too extreme, and so a solution would be found somewhere in the compromise between the two. He suggested that the son of the Evenkii spend two days embracing his tree bride and then spend two days apart from her, alternating in this way between sweet and sour until the perfect blend was reached and the bride would be saved.

The son of the Evenkii was not certain whose advice to heed, so he resolved to perform each of their tasks in turn.

Upon his return to the Old Fen, he first soaked his bride's roots in the honey given to him by The Lady, who told him it came from the hives of the ancient jungles of the Warampi. Their hives grew to sizes larger than the mudbrick homes of the Evenkii, and the price of their honey was so that it would take many lifetimes to earn enough for a spoonful.

The son of the Evenkii waited and searched for any sign of life in the bark of his bride's face.

Weeks yet, and there was nothing.

But the son of the Evenkii wasn't deterred. He then gathered his effects and departed the Old Fen, returning to his home in the land of the Evenkii. He helped in the fields and with the construction of homes to pass the time, but he marked the days carefully so he would not keep his bride waiting too long should she emerge from her bark cocoon. And when it was time, he came back to her.

And she was there, still frozen in her wooden form.

So, the son of the Evenkii did as The Aged suggested, and spent his days alternating between embracing his bride and withdrawing from her presence. But weeks of this routine also yielded nothing.

His bride remained a tree.

The son of the Evenkii refused to relent, even in that desperate circumstance.

He sat in front of his bride and waited—for hope, for an answer, for anything.

And in the silence came the solution.

The son of the Evenkii sat in front of his bride and listened. He listened, and then he heard the somber song emanating from beneath the black bark. The longer he listened, the louder her song became, and the roughness of her new form softened until at last the daughter of the Irtysh emerged.

She sang to him of her pain, and he listened.

And when she had emptied herself before him, the son of the Evenkii embraced the daughter of the Irtysh, his beloved bride, swearing that he would always hold her close, protect her, and listen to her until his time was done.

The new blooms of ivy crept along the white marble of the Academy, a covert soldier in enemy territory right before the dawn. For years it suffered in a stalemate of determination between it and its foe—the units of people who wrenched its body away from the structure it sought to overtake. But as it crawled over the central dome that towered above the landscape of Somewhere, it sensed a shift in the delicate threads of the cosmic and pushed forward in glee.

There was nothing that could be done, but still Ellis scrubbed. Blood blossomed from fresh wounds on her neck and thigh, and even more pooled between her legs. She wept as she recalled her mother advising her some time before about how red was the color of womanhood, that one day she would bloom and paint her lips and be grown. But slumped over her oddly crossed legs watching droplets of blood sprout and draw slim lines across her skin, she didn't feel like she had come to some great stage in her life. Ellis instead believed she belonged in the red robes of the grave-maids, for she felt closer to death than anything else.

The iron disappeared under the canvas of bright blood, and that was some relief at least. It would not last, she knew, but for that small measure of time, red gave her peace.

Discarded sculptures lay in pieces scattered about the cosmic floor beneath Time's desk. In their remains, phantoms of beauty peered out from broken halves. Planetary bodies and celestial sands swirled around him, but Time was so fixed on his mark that he noticed nothing except the slide of his fingertips against each new material, fashioning parts that were once of the Nothing into something just for him.

Something that would last.

And in his zeal, Death was forgotten. She chewed her fingers and tapped the lips of empty jars against her brother's desk, her belly as empty as the hollow containers. With some interest, she watched as Time crafted elegant forms and curse at himself once the work was complete. Another shapely figurine would be smashed against the floor of the universe, pieces flying to all corners of the endless realm of galaxies.

But eventually, there came a day when Time thought he had fashioned the perfect companion, and he gazed upon the visage of the Young, a spring eternal that would never wither. And in the chaos of his euphoria, Death saw opportunity. Hungry and forsaken, her passion propelled her forward, and her great mouth devoured Time's companion as well as his hands.

The biting sting of betrayal was far worse than the severing of limbs.

Time produced a pair of crude hands, molding them with the ashes of a supernova using the jagged stumps of what was left of his wrists. They were imperfect—too thin and knobby—as he now was. And in his fury, he wielded his new hands against Death, who was transformed into black holes distributed throughout the cosmos.

Time's titan body wracked with sobs, mourning Death, the loss of his creator's hands, and the destruction of his lovely companion who would never sit at his side while he brought miracles into being. He worried that his hands would never again shape the perfect, but that would not keep him from trying.

When came the time for the mothers of the Council to approach the Headmaster, they painted their lips and wore their brightest floral dresses for the occasion. They floated to the Academy bearing baskets of honeyed treats, believing that most problems could be solved with a bit of sweetness.

But they left the Academy that day as unsuccessful as the elders before them, their baskets still in hand. The honeyed treats untouched. The mothers murmured to one another that next would come the workmen, and they prayed that their skilled hands and simple knowledge could unknot the tangle at the Academy.

Their children had yet to come home, and their chance to contend with Time was slipping between their fingers. They returned to their looms at the Council House and weaved the day's account into the newest tapestry.

Ellis ate.

Ellis attended lessons.

Ellis joined her friends at the river when the warmth of spring blew across Somewhere.

Ellis showered.

Ellis listened to Ofelia's stories.

Ellis scrubbed at the iron patches until blood spilled over her skin.

Ellis felt peace.

Ellis felt numb.

Ellis was led into a dim office by fingers that pillaged and razed her body.

Ellis was lost in the rhythms of this new normal, swept along without any mooring sense of agency that was entirely her own.

Ellis held Kal's hand but did not feel it.

Ellis held Ofelia's hand but did not feel it.

Ellis resisted the Headmaster's hands. He delighted in her red blossoming.

Ellis was a woman. That's what her mother said.

Ellis was a woman now. That's what the Headmaster said.

Ellis stopped scrubbing her iron patches bloody, finally understanding that red wasn't peace.

It was ruin.

The dizzying effects of

a first kiss

The frenzied scratching of pencil on paper was somewhat soothing to Ellis. It was the first time in weeks she'd heard anything other than her own thoughts. Nox glanced at Ellis over the thick frames of his glasses and sighed.

"At some point, you will actually have to pick up your pencil." Though his expression was severe, his tone was soft. It made Ellis wince.

She had grown wary of that combination.

Pencil in hand, Ellis stared at the paper in front of her. The mass of numbers blurred as her frustration mounted. Who cared about calculations right now?

As tears welled, Nox scooted his chair closer to hers. "It's not that difficult once you get the hang of it. Here," he said as he sat next to her, solving the equation with ease. "Understand?"

Ellis shook her head, the salt water in her eyes threatening to spill over.

Nox studied her for a moment, then propped his head up with his fist, his glasses shifting. "El—have you talked to Kal? Or Rowan?"

Ellis looked at Nox pleadingly and whispered, "I... I can't."

Silence engulfed them, thickening the musty air in the library to the point it became suffocating. It was only the jovial murmurs of students passing or idly gossiping at tables some distance from them that broke the quiet trance. Ellis wiped her eyes on the sleeves of her oversized sweater.

"Only this once and on one condition." Nox's held his pencil mere inches above Ellis' homework. Ellis sniffled. "I know you won't talk to me, but at least talk to Kal. Surely you've noticed that he's not been himself either?"

Ellis froze. Talk to Kal? How could she? Would the words even form on her tongue? "I'll try."

"That isn't good enough, Ellis. We're all pretty mystified by your strange behavior, but Kal is well and truly suffering for it. He barely eats or sleeps, and his lessons have all but been ignored as well. Is there… Is there something going on between the two of you?"

That isn't good enough. Ellis knew his intentions weren't wicked, but those words closed around her like a fist. Suddenly she exploded, "I am trying, Nox! I'm trying, I'm trying, I'm trying! You have no idea…"

Nox was stunned but reacted quickly, true to form. "Then tell me! Say something, Ellis. Say anything! We are trying too, but we are moving in darkness."

Every eye in the library was drawn to the pair, desperate to know what was happening between them. Ellis was crying freely now, tears cutting rivers across her face. Under the weight of his thick lashes, she swore she saw relief. Nox believed the dam had burst. He reached out to her and covered her hand with his.

It was warm, and Ellis tried not to crumble.

He said nothing else, just slid her paper with his free hand closer to him and started writing. The watchful gazes of the other students quickly found other things to occupy and entertain them. Ellis laid her head on the table, drowsily observing Nox as he worked.

He squeezed her hand gently, a gesture that reminded her of Kal.

She fell asleep listening to the scratching of pencil on paper as she carefully repaired the damage in the dam wall.

Thoughts on time, the second. **An echo.**

Where does the past go to live? Is it carried solely in the memories of all species only to be destroyed piece by piece as Death visits, or is there some wondrous place in the universe where the past has made a home?

Discoveries made over and over again.

Wars on an endless loop.

The sweetest moments replayed and never vanishing.

A place where I could snuggle into the arms of my grandmother and never let go.

Ellis was once a silent child. Neither of her parents nor any of her friends could make her speak when she was younger, and after trying everything they could possibly think of to get her to talk and failing, they resigned themselves to loving her mute.

Her grandmother came to visit her one afternoon from her home at the Council House when Ellis was eight. The mothers of Somewhere were the only ones who were part of the Council who also served as grave-maids. Mothers were tied to both life and to death, and as such, held a singular space on the Council.

The day she visited, she and Ellis worked together in the family's garden, wrenching out weeds and pressing their fingers into soft earth.

Her grandmother then asked her, "Is there nothing for which you want to speak?"

Ellis looked at her grandmother, her small frame and warm expression, and shook her head.

Her grandmother smiled and handed her a flower bud to plant. "One day, Ellis, there will be something you want to say, because it will be important. One day, Ellis, you're going to have to scream for it, because silence is nothing, and you are very much something."

245

A heatwave visited before anyone in Somewhere had opportunity to prepare. Student and instructor alike languished in the unbearably thick air inside the Academy walls, fanning themselves with folded notes as sweat pooled in the dips and shallows of their bodies under their attire. Open mouths breathed heavy sighs in attempts to expel heat from their insides, but they only succeeded in bouts of dizziness. Ellis pressed her cheek against the cool wood of the desk, delighting in the shock of the sensation until it vanished, succumbing to the heat of her skin.

The students were dismissed when the instructor found that she could barely concentrate, her chalk script failing at coherency as she struggled to focus on the topic at hand.

Red and gray was stripped away, and the children raced to the river.

The sounds of splashing, relief, and laughter cut through the heavy air, but Ellis wouldn't join in the jubilation. Her friends would be there. Kal would be there. And she was not ready. Not yet. She crossed the lawn of the Academy to its foregarden barefoot, the soft grass tickling the spaces between her toes. A bloom of red curls lay upon the ground, attached to the most exuberant being Ellis had ever encountered.

She smiled.

"Not interested in the river either?" Ellis asked as she approached.

When Ofelia shifted to look at her, Ellis nearly gasped aloud. Her once bright eyes barely shined, as dimly lit as the office of the Headmaster. And they were sunken, as her frame was sunken, almost as if she were collapsing in on herself like a dying star.

Ellis fell to her knees beside the crumpling figure.

"Not today. Today I wanted to be somewhere quiet." When Ellis glanced at her worryingly, Ofelia said, "But you can lay beside me. I think you're the only person in the whole world whose company I'd like right now." She smiled, but it, too, was diminished.

Ellis melted into the grass, their arms kissing, their hair mingling. The heat warmed their faces, and they closed their eyes in the bright light of the midday sun.

"Tell me a story?" Ellis asked, looking at Ofelia through the blackness behind her eyelids.

An excruciating pause, then Ofelia's fingers slid between hers, her palm moist from the hellish heat. "Not today," she repeated. "Today I only want to exist in this moment. It's peaceful, isn't it?"

Ellis nodded, though she wasn't sure Ofelia saw it.

Seconds stretched, overtaking minutes and hours. The pair lived in those seconds, listening as hot air was cycled through their lungs and their hearts beat a steady rhythm behind their ribcages. Ellis felt Ofelia move, and then a tug on her fingers.

She opened her eyes and saw red curls casting a sweet face in shadows. Ellis sat up with her, and her pulse thrummed only once before Ofelia's lips met hers, the taste of milk chocolate exploding in her mouth.

Ofelia pulled away slowly.

Ellis' pulse vibrated again. "W-why?"

She dizzied in the wake of heat and chocolate.

Ofelia's blue-green eyes met Ellis' black ones, serious-ness creeping across her face. "Today I needed to kiss someone I care about. Someone who cares about me."

Ellis groped for words that would not come, and Ofelia took two chocolates from her pocket, the red and gold wrappers bright in the light of the sun. She gave one to Ellis and popped the other in her mouth after unwrap-ping it carefully, the chocolate already partially melted and misshapen.

The raven-haired girl watched as the red-haired girl gripped her legs and put her chin on her knees.

"Today I have this, Ellis. Today is what you've given me."

The chocolate lingering on her tastebuds gave way to something bitter, something sour like vinegar. Ellis pushed her chocolate between her lips, hoping to chase away the unwelcome flavor, but it conquered the incoming sweetness and settled into her like a stubborn stain.

Thoughts on love, the second. **An echo.**

Trapped behind a cage of bones and squished between two oversized, bean-shaped organs is the heart. The engine pumps life steadily throughout the body, relentless in its endeavor. Stories and holidays and parents say it is the seat of love, and so its image has been scrawled in journals, carved into trees, and replicated in art for a portion of human history. And though we know better thanks to the great minds that have worked out how human emotions are formed and processed in the brain, we continue to believe in the myth.

Is it because it has so pervaded our society that we cannot wrest it from its place, or could it be for convenience's sake, or perhaps it stems from a more romantical desire to keep the heart on its throne as the place of love since books with lines like, "I love you with all my brain," fall hopelessly short of the impact it needs?

Maybe there is another reason altogether, one which

comes from experience. You see, while the great minds have astounding evidence that love comes from the brain, it is not the brain that skips when you fall in love, and it is not the brain that aches when you're heartbroken.

It has always been the heart.

Alone in the dark of a room, a young girl with apple-skin curls wrote a story in a letter from memory.

It was from the old epic she'd never recovered but couldn't forget.

It was a story that gave her the determination to seek her freedom.

She kissed the folded edge of the letter, now shaped like an envelope, and put two chocolates in red and gold wrappers side by side on top of it.

She smiled as she popped the cap off a large jug of vinegar, and kept smiling as she poured it all down her throat.

Crumbling isn't just a

verb

Kal was nowhere to be found. Nox hadn't seen him come to lessons or on the field for any games, and Rowan, always taking the initiative, had the Academy staff let her into his room so that she could look for him.

But he wasn't there.

The entire grounds were meticulously and exhaustively searched by the group, and it was only by chance that Ellis came upon him as she entered the one place she swore she'd never go again.

His black locks were even messier than usual, and there was something about the way he stared absently at something unseen by Ellis that unnerved her. It was the same expression Ofelia had worn the last she saw her. Broken.

She didn't know if he was aware of her presence, but she marched forward and wrapped her arms around

253

his stomach, leaning her head against his back between his shoulder blades.

He needed her, and so she would have to be strong.

Kal's body tensed, then Ellis felt the soft vibrations of crying through his skin.

"Do you love her, Ellis? That girl?"

The question was like an arrow fired through her spine.

He knew. He had seen, or someone had and told him. It didn't really matter which.

"I...don't know." It was all she could say, but it was true.

Kal and Ellis fell to their knees together, still holding on to one another.

Kal's seafoam eyes were overfull of tears. "And me? Do you love me?"

"Yes." Ellis slid the crown of her head under the crook of Kal's neck, the safest port she'd ever known.

His fingers surfed the calm of her thin hair, grasping a section tightly, then released it. And with the ease of his tension, came a question: "I need to know, Ellis. Please."

There was no need for specifics.

This moment had been reaching for Ellis like the hands of Time.

And like Kal, she had been rigid, needing the release. So, she tried to release it.

All of it.

And then she crumbled.

Thoughts on life, the third. An echo.

How do you begin to measure a life?

Is there a cosmic scale to weigh the value of your atoms, actions, and agonies? And would you be weighed against yourself or weighed against others?

If a person is the vessel of a billion moving parts, can there actually be an accurate formula to determine a person's worth?

In all cases, even the most objective answer is sub-jective. Everything dependent upon perspective and shaped by experience.

So how do you begin to measure a life?

There was a rumor among the ancient tribes that the man of the Old Fen returned to his ramshackle cabin long after the grandchildren of the son of the Even-kii and the daughter of the Irtysh passed into the next life, but not a soul was bold enough to venture there to confirm, though a single column of smoke was seen rising between the treetops of the Old Fen most nights.

Families huddled closer, and some even went so far as to stitch the edges of their clothes together so that all members remained close throughout the days and the nights. For if the man was indeed there, they refused to lose any beloved to his strange greed.

A few months after the ancient tribes noticed the smoke, it suddenly disappeared. They watched the treetops for days, anxiously waiting to see if it would return. When it didn't, a few of their strongest went forth to investigate.

The ramshackle cabin still stood, though no light at all shined inside. It was utterly empty. The strongest of the ancient tribes relaxed, happy that the man was gone and they could return to peace in their villages.

Then they saw the trees.

Where once were black willow trees with features of creatures once human, there was nothing except ruin,

257

as if the humans had been harshly severed from the willows by the blunt edge of an angry axe. All that remained of them was bits of wood pulp scattered around the roots of the trees, children lost forever to the forest floor.

The strongest of the ancient tribes became ill at the sight and fled from the Old Fen, failing to notice the spot where once had been the willow form of the daughter of the Irtysh, the ground now adorned with roses, the flowers of the dead.

The Council of Somewhere had abandoned their work, instead spending their days measuring the inches the ground had sunk beneath them each night. It was as if Somewhere had suddenly found itself in the gravity of a black hole, and its dark maw was drawing them in bit by bit toward the singularity underneath the Garden, eager for its taste of Utopia the Council once firmly believed they'd built.

They stood at their looms and their books, feeling no sense of creation in their fingers.

But they knew hopelessness for the first time.

For even Fates must bow down to Time and Death when they come to visit.

4.

(it isn't.)

The tragedy of Ofelia

Ellis hated endings. How could anything ever really be properly concluded? There were always things left unsaid, questions unanswered, secrets lurking in dark corners like wispy cobwebs. Endings were too fixed. Too final. Too permanent.

But there was a finale of some sort galloping toward her like a stampede, except individuals had broken off from the bulk of the herd, clipping her randomly until she wasn't certain how long the ending would last, or if she were actually already in it.

She thought expiration would arrive swiftly when she found Kal in the Garden.

But it hadn't.

He had needed her to speak, to say something.

But she didn't.

Not anything real anyway. Not absolute truth, but a road parallel to it.

"I'm just not okay."

He had drawn her face into his chest and she felt his heart's steady rhythm against her lips, and if Ellis could have pried open the cage of his ribs to plant a kiss on that all-important muscular organ, she would have, if only to soothe his concern over their recent lack of closeness.

Someday her tongue and lips and teeth would form the words she needed to say.

But it wasn't that day.

And it hasn't been the day since.

Kal's hand still found hers, and now she wouldn't let go.

Thoughts on time, the third. An echo.

All things are eternal borrowers, too many of them fervent in their prayers of thanks to the countless gods who've emerged and evaporated across eons, never imagining that Time and Death are the true gods to which creatures owe their gratitude.

Time is said to sow all things and feeds all things to Death, an endless labor of devotion and care to his sister, whose appetite is never satisfied.

And we, these temporary beasts of the universe, are as miniature replicas of Death's form—our greedy mouths devouring seconds, minutes, and hours as they pass through us, always desperate for more.

Could it then be said that Time is a selfless god?

Is there nothing to be gained from his acts, or are we missing something?

Something important.

Something urgent.

Something we are overlooking with our mouths wide, consuming seconds, minutes, and hours with barely a thought given to the process, outcome, or motive.

The silence in the Council House was as oppressive as the presence of Time or the threat of Death. The looms no longer creaked with the movement of the wefts, the books no longer being bound and unbound, the inkwells were nearly dried out. The mothers and the elders had failed in their efforts, so now all was left to the workmen, who lingered in the dark rooms of the Council House carving shapes from broken looms and carving a strategy from the unused pieces of ideas lurking in the dark rooms of their minds.

The elders' tactic was forceful, but not severe.

The mothers' sweetness had no impact.

All that was left was the extreme, the sourest approach.

The workmen sat carving their shapes and waited for Death.

Grief wasn't a dead thing. It thrived, roosting in your chest, growing fat on loss.

Loss.

Lossttt.

She was losst.

Ofelia's lips were eroded. Her once bright eyes were milky and frozen. The bloom of red curls framing her face was without its shine.

Scattered around her body like an enormous halo were rumpled red and gold chocolate wrappers. To her left were three empty vinegar jugs.

Stale urine stained the floor below her stiff legs, mixing with a pool of spilled vinegar.

Ellis couldn't breathe.

Grief sat like a vulture in the room with Ellis and the body, taking note of her dimensions, planning its destructive entrance the instant Ellis took a breath. She couldn't hold it forever.

She wanted to hold it forever.

She wanted to hold Ofelia forever.

She ground her teeth until her jaw cracked and her gums bled, fighting against the blossoming ache in her chest, but she was no fighter. No warrior. That had been Ofelia.

That's what she believed anyway.

And with her exhalation, Grief rushed gleefully forward and devoured her, and there were no units to preserve her, no one to pluck at the creeping vines of Grief as it swallowed her. And as it clutched her soft tissues and tendons, Ellis swept Ofelia's body up into her arms, screaming into the swoops of her curls as the scent of salt water and vinegar conquered the atmosphere in Ofelia's room.

She didn't notice when figures in white robes burst into the room.

She didn't notice when they circled her, still clinging to Ofelia.

But when they separated the girls, Ellis noticed.

When they lifted Ofelia and a patch of gray peeked out from under her shirt, Ellis noticed.

She was slipping, disappearing into loss.

Losst.

The Headmaster's Story according to the elders of Somewhere, who wrote their account in an old epic alongside other accounts of his history, and abandoned it in the Great Library of the Academy, knowing one day it would be needed by a tiny girl with apple-skin curls:

We knew his form, his shape and shadow, his purpose.

Time had wandered into our sanctuary, our Somewhere, looking for something that endures.

Something forever.

And we knew what needed to be done.

The accelerating

erosion of gold

Sometimes events aren't like waves breaking upon a shore. Sometimes they are more like two liquids of differing densities poured into the same bowl. Whatever their unique elements and composition, everything in the bowl will swirl and overlap and blend until you can hardly tell one from the other, especially in the moment of the action. Only when comes the cessation of all kinetic energy—the hollow valley in between the moments of action—do the liquids separate and settle. And in that valley of calm, you can see the events as individual entities, and more importantly, determine which ones caused you most damage by how low the memories of them sink into your chest.

Scraping the bottom of Ellis' was the image of Ofelia's eroded mouth and lifeless eyes.

She had cried until there was nothing left in her to express and slept until her muscles could take no more stagnation.

There was a bowl of some sort of porridge on the misshapen table beside the bed where she lay. Ellis didn't have to touch it to know that it was cold. The grim-faced elder who'd brought it to her that morning sniffed at her other untouched plates, gathered them up silently, and left the room without so much as poking at the girl-shaped lump under the blankets to check that she was indeed still living.

But she supposed she was.

That is, if this state she was in could actually be called living.

They had brought Ellis here to the Council House after... Well, *after*. It would all be after now, wouldn't it? Everything carefully measured by whether it came before or following the moment Ofelia was nothing more than the cage of sinew and veins in which all that was her had once resided—a book with all of its pages ripped out. No stories. No life. Nothing except the binding.

They brought her here wearing their white robes and unconcerned expressions like armor and questioned her until she thought there could be no shadowed corner of her life unknown to them. Then they saw the iron patches blooming on her skin, their apathy quickly morphing into anxiety, and put her in a little room in a tower of the Council House, somewhere above the musty rooms where the Council sat at looms and books and mess, making and unmaking the great tales of Somewhere.

There she stayed. For however long, she wasn't sure, for she would not leave the sanctuary of her bed to look for sunlight or moonlight. Under those heavy blankets, she could fall into the Nothing. For in the Nothing, this ache in her chest did not exist.

And while she melted into oblivion, the corners of the golden statues in the garden began to crack and flake away, revealing a dull, gray iron underneath.

Thoughts on time, the first. An echo.

Time is a hell of a thing. It shuffles everything along, willing or not, toward ruin with absolute indifference.

I once wrote a list of things Time has taken from me when I was much younger, but as so often happens, it was also lost to Time, that ever-reaping force.

Or I might have lost it somewhere in the mess in my room I haven't yet bothered to clean.

Fluctuat nec mergitur

Whispers had a way of sounding menacing even when they didn't mean to. This was particularly true when you were the audience to them rather than a partic- ipant. No matter the prowess of your reasoning, it collapsed in the wake of muttered secrets you were certain were about you. Ellis slumped over her knees on the creaking, ancient bed, straining to hear the conversation in the hallway between elders without moving an inch. She caught a few errant words in the din of murmurs, but nothing stood out until there was mention of a burial.

Ellis knew immediately whose burial it was, and she drove her nose between her knees to muffle her cries. Another person she hopelessly adored was going into the ground, planted like a root under pounds of dirt, surrounded by roses and streaked faces. And then Time would take Ofelia's body, calling upon the worms and insects and minerals to erode her to dust, to nothing. Ellis tried desperately to recall the sound of her voice as she spoke animatedly about some book or other, or how the freckles smattered across her nose always

resembled a scrambling of constellations, but everything was fuzzy, as if she were trying to see things
through a fogged window.

The whispers suddenly ceased, and the door to her
darkened room was flung open, the elder standing
in the doorway bearing the weight of urgency in his
expression. "I am sorry to disturb you, Ellis, but the
Headmaster is gone."

Ellis blinked, feeling a wound tearing open at the
mention of his name. "W-what?"

The elder's face softened, and he grabbed the wobbly
stool by the door and brought it to the bed, dropping
onto it without even striving for grace. "I'm afraid so.
He disappeared shortly after..."

After.

It would all be after now, wouldn't it?

"...and we've searched the grounds as well as all areas
surrounding the river, but he has not been found."

Somewhere inside of her body, Ellis felt her cells disin-
tegrating, and a heavy breath slid shakily between
her lips. It was impossible for the Headmaster to have
disappeared when she felt his predatory presence in

every stone-stacked wall of her room and could hear the buttered tone of his voice lurking in the forgotten places in her mind and still sensed the pressure of his palms on her skin. It stung her that his elements could be recalled without effort when Ellis was fighting to hold on to every scrap of Ofelia.

"Ellis?" the elder asked expectantly, his eyes near swallowed by wrinkles as he studied her. "Are you all right?"

"I..." *All right. What is that anyway?*

His silvery, long hair—a trademark of the elders— was braided loosely, a style not typically favored of the elders. He reached for her, then stopped himself. "I am sorry, Ellis, for all of it. I feel had we done something much sooner..." His hand returned to his lap. "Ofelia is being carried by the gravemaids to rest today. Do you...want to go?"

Another strange word. *Want.* There was no want here, no desire existing inside of her that wanted to see Ofelia as a body, not as herself. But she *had* to go. Perhaps, that word was more appropriate. Ellis couldn't not go, no matter how much it would pick at the wound festering in her chest. She would go and see Ofelia. She would go and say goodbye.

Ellis nodded.

He smiled, a gentle smile, and pulled something from his pocket. "Also, we found this in Ofelia's room. We thought you might want it."

A letter folded like an envelope, concealing two chocolates in red and gold wrappers and a story. Ellis pushed the chocolates into her mouth and cried what she believed were the last reserves of her tears as she read the story of a fierce warrior who defied a king with strange hands and sought her freedom in death, written in Ofelia's beautiful script.

***

The cool winds carried the song of the dead sung by the red-garbed gravemaids, mothers of the Council. It floated through Somewhere, wholly indifferent to the threatening storm clouds overhead, and found Ellis as she walked to the necropolis alone. The elder and his kin had offered to escort her, but she refused. Their company did not bring her any comfort nor sense of safety. Even if the Headmaster wasn't actually standing in front of her, he was still with her. They could not spare her that.

No one could. Right?

And then a familiar hand found hers and squeezed, and a rush of tears spilled from her eyes. Kal pulled Ellis into his arms and she wrapped hers around him, grabbing large fistfuls of his shirt as she cried against his heart. He kissed the crown of her head and rested his chin there, rocking her in his embrace until he was sure she was ready to let go.

The gravemaids moved in two neat rows, carrying between them on a wooden litter Ofelia's body, covered in a cream cloth and roses. Kal and Ellis followed them, and she said goodbye to Ofelia.

That night, Ellis returned to Ofelia's grave and tore away the roses.

Thoughts on love, the third. **An echo.**

Humans are conquering creatures. They skulk about in the open, determining weaknesses in their quarry, and when they strike, it is to destroy or bring to heel. They plant flags in foreign earth, believing whole-heartedly that this odd act affords them dominion. They abduct their kin and label them "less than" for reasons that hold as much water as a bucket without a bottom.

Control makes them feel powerful. Control makes them feel as if they are turning the tide against Time's command, even if for a little while.

It is peculiar then that humans should put so much of their focus outward, when a squishy bag that pumps blood squatting in their bodies that influences their lives so heavily is permitted to continue doing so.

Weird creatures indeed.

The ivy was not yet satisfied, and so slinked forward, its hunger to swallow the Academy propelling its efforts. It knocked at the marble until it cracked, and squeezed the tops of the towers until they began to crumble in its tendrilled grasp. Still, not one of those in Somewhere noticed, and not one came to clear away the conquering vines, for they were so weighted by their sorrow that they trudged through the days and nights as if their flesh had suddenly become made of that selfsame heavy stone of the vanquished ivory structure.

And in their leaden states, the same question lingered on everyone's lips.

"Where is the Headmaster?"

The Garden's atmosphere grew dense, and its gravity intensified to such a degree that Ellis found herself yanked toward its precipice, as if it meant to devour her. The roses were in full bloom, splotches of blood against the gold of the statues. And it was then that Ellis noticed a fraying of the gold, revealing traces of iron peeking through the fissures.

She touched the iron patch on her neck and froze.

"I had such hopes for them, but I couldn't make them last."

Soft butter on a warm tongue.

At the tip of her index finger, Ellis felt a thread unravel from her flesh, pulled toward the belly of the Garden.

His black eyes met her own, and he reached for her hand, tugging it away from her neck. "It will not be your fate, Ellis. I know I can make you last. I want you to last. I want you to sit with me forever." His slender fingers glided around her neck, his thumb tracing circles over the grayed skin. "I have been alone for so long."

Ellis shook, her lips trembling as his gaze held her in place. The thread of flesh from her finger unwound faster, twisting around her muscles until she couldn't feel her left arm anymore. She was disappearing, the Garden's gravity eating her up.

"Come with me, Ellis. Come, let's leave," the Headmaster said, but it was not a request. "I cannot stay here any longer, and I cannot bear to leave you. I would have time to perfect this," he gestured to the iron on her skin, "and you could sit by me forever." Ellis stopped breathing. "You are so like her. So like my sister. Two quiet little things who are not quiet at all inside. I hear you in there, Ellis."

A question formed in her middle. Its components welded together and moved up, up through her esophagus so forcefully that Ellis scarcely had opportunity to resist it. And only when the question had escaped between her lips, its parts wholly intact, did she realize it was the only question that mattered at all. "Did…did you do this to Ofelia too?"

If the question surprised him, the Headmaster did not show it. His face, altogether too beautiful for a destructive being such as he, remained ever fixed in its conquering expression. He was a creature of take, and he had taken far too much from Ellis.

People who mattered.

"I thought I sensed something in her, something like

I sense in you. But it wasn't there. She didn't want to sit at my side, and she wasn't like my sister at all." His hand left Ellis' neck and took hold of her arm. "Ofelia was never meant to last."

It is a strange sort of sensation to be told an answer which you already guessed, especially when the confirmation of that answer is something that shatters you, molecules and all. Ellis' body wracked with sobs, and the ground underneath her feet shuddered.

Nothing was steady.

Nothing was forever.

And it was in that realization that Ellis didn't find peace, as some tend to do in turmoil, but found riot instead. *"One day, Ellis, there will be something you want to say, because it will be important. One day, Ellis, you're going to have to scream for it, because silence is nothing, and you are very much something."* So she screamed, a shriek so loud and melancholy and furious that the sinking soil shifted and broke, tearing across the Garden with the urgency of a tide swept up in the wind. In the center of the Garden the earth opened up, pulling down the roses and the greenery and the statues into the dark belly of Death.

It consumed the Headmaster, who tumbled into the

black while reaching out for Ellis with inhuman hands.

But she wasn't devoured.

Ellis was pulled from that crumbling place by a wholly different force. Kal had grabbed her and pulled her away from the widening black hole gulping down this patch of Somewhere. He let her scream as everything vanished in front of them, and he listened to all of it.

Then together, they watched as Death swallowed the Garden whole.

Squeeze

A list of things Time has taken from me.

~~My favorite purple spotted boots I outgrew last summer.~~

~~All of my baby teeth.~~

~~Each of my memories before I was five.~~

People who matter.

Death had become more than simply a creature of destruction. Like her brother, she used the eons scattered across the cosmos to cultivate a new skill. However, unlike Time, she had no use for creation, save for the purpose it served to satisfy her never-ending hunger. The great titan of devouring chose to sharpen her skills of observation.

She watched from the singularities in which her brother had banished her to, forever a swirling vortex of obliteration, and seethed as he moved through the ages, reaping one soul after another, forever searching for that which he already once had.

Was it not her that sat with him in the long hours of the work?

Her that nibbled on stardust while he coaxed the seconds, minutes, and hours of all things?

Her that sat together with him in the Nothing before he made all of the somethings?

It was supposed to be just for her. Wasn't it?

Why create if not to destroy?

But Time, well, he had wanted something to last, hadn't he?

Death had.

And she would wait and watch. And then she would swallow him whole.

Reunited at last, eternally.

Thoughts on life, the first. **An echo.**

Hell if I know.

When the Council sifted through the Headmaster's office, they discovered the old epic lying on an end table, barely visible in the dim light of the room. They opened the book and saw that there were several pages missing. Horrified at its crude cleaving, the mothers spirited the book away to the safety of the Council House while the elders and workmen drew back the heavy curtains of the Headmaster's office to let the light in.

Even in their most tragic moments, humans can be marvelously resilient.

The people of Somewhere didn't permit the Academy to succumb to the ivy. Each day, a unit of the people came and tugged at the green invader, feeling lighter with each discarded vine. But they knew the ivy would persist. It, like Grief, was a relentless force that needed to be plucked away piece by piece until Time reaped it, like it does all things.

Ellis and Kal and their friends joined the units after she had given Ofelia's handwritten story to the Council, knowing that the tale of the fierce warrior who defied the king and sought her freedom in death didn't belong to her. The Council restitched it into the recovered epic, finally making it whole again, and returned it to the library. The thought of it made Ellis smile, for she knew how happy it would have made Ofelia to know that the epic might one day find its way to another who needed it. And for the first time, the Council members left their dusty home, abandoning their tapestries and their books, and dirtied their hands with their people, ready to join in the long hours of the work of creation from destruction.

The iron patches remained. Perhaps they would remain forever, but for the first time Ellis didn't feel the need to hide them. Her friends embraced her, knowing that one day she would feel strong enough to tell them everything she needed to, for she had found the loud spirit inside of her.

And every now and then, Kal would take her hand and squeeze.

About the Author

Ashley Hutchison

Editor, writer, and painter, with experience working for Triplicity Publishing, New London Writers, and Jorvik Press. She is editor-in-chief of Lost Boys Press, and when not dabbling in books and art, you'll find Ashley searching for the weird and wonderful in local bookstores.

www.lostboyspress.com

Also available from Lost Boys Press

Novellas:

A Map to the Stars by Ashley Hutchison
The Garden of the Golden Children by Ashley Hutchison

Full Length:

Ghost River by Chad Ryan

Anthologies:

Chimera
Not Meant for Each Other
Heroes

E-Zines:

Bloom
Storm
Ignite
Moot
Doom

CPSIA information can be obtained
at www.ICGtesting.com
Printed in the USA
JSHW042034021022
31243JS00004B/8/J